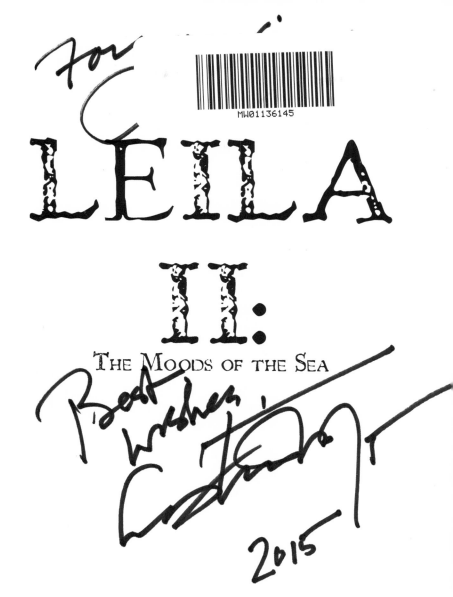

For C[...]

LEILA

II:

THE MOODS OF THE SEA

Best wishes,
[signature]
2015

HEATHER NEFF

Printed in the United States of America
ISBN: 1499775350
EAN-13: 9781499775358
Library of Congress Control Number: 2014913566
CreateSpace Independent Publishing Platform
North Charleston, South Carolina
Visit www.amazon.com and other retail outlets to
order additional copies.

Leila II: The Moods of the Sea

Leila, the twelve-year-old daughter of illiterate parents, spent her childhood in a mud hut in the Atlas Mountains of Morocco. Given to three strangers in payment for her father's debts, she is forced to work in a brothel before being sold to a wealthy, prominent man.

Leila: the Weighted Silence of Memory recounts Leila's years of physical, sexual, and emotional abuse at the hands of her captors. After managing to escape, she seeks to rebuild her life with a family suffering from tragic losses of their own.

Leila II: The Moods of the Sea finds Leila three years later, still a fugitive from the man who held her captive. Though deeply haunted by her past and her fear of recapture, her hard work has brought fortune to the family that shelters her. As they try to better their lives with a new business venture, Leila takes her first steps toward healing. Her world gains new meaning when she is drawn toward a powerful, unexpected love.

After a terrible coincidence delivers her again into the hands of her tormenters, Leila suffers a vicious assault that leaves her body broken. Now she must fight for herself, her future – and for everyone and everything she has come to care for.

A tale of human trafficking, Leila's story illuminates the plight of more than twelve million victims held in modern-day slavery throughout the world.

Praise for *Leila: The Weighted Silence of Memory*

"*Leila* is brave, compelling fiction that speaks many truths about a subject fraught with silence and denial. Moments of human connection, hope and resistance punctuate Leila's descent into increasing domination and despair. The nuanced characters are true to their context, and the tactics and justifications of Leila's oppressors, as well as the physical and emotional scars they cause, exist across religions and nations that have substantial economic and gender inequality.

— Dr. Paul Leighton, Ph.D.

Neff, a supremely gifted writer, captures the reader with words so engaging it is as if you're being held hostage by this sorrowful tale as it blooms into a story of hope."

— Cassandra Spratling, *The Detroit Free Press*

Leila: The Weighted Silence of Memory is poignant, although tragic, and masterfully written...

— Amazon reader

Heather Neff is a professor of English and the author of seven books, including *Wisdom*, designated an Honor Book by the Black Caucus of the American Library Association, *Haarlem, Accident of Birth, Blackgammon,* and *Leila: The Weighted Silence of Memory*. Educated at the University of Michigan and the University of Paris, Neff earned her Ph.D. at the University of Zurich, in Switzerland. The recipient of numerous teaching awards, Neff currently serves as Director of the McNair Scholars Program at Eastern Michigan University. Neff was named a 2007 Michigan Distinguished Professor by the Presidents Council.

Neff enjoys painting in acrylics, biking, walking, and participating in a variety of community activities in her spare time.

Visit her website at: www.heatheneffbooks.com

For Aviva Helena
and
Alma Marie

...it is better to speak
remembering
we were never meant to survive

— Audre Lorde, "A Litany for Survival"

Silence is the door of consent.

— Berber proverb

Prologue

January 29, 2014

17:02

They came for me just as the boy, face still rosy with sleep, wrapped his arms around my knees.

The sun had etched her path across the marble tables, and now stained the floor through the scarlet glass above the door. The tearoom was empty, for we were too near the dinner hour for women to linger over *ghoribas* and spearmint tea. Indeed, the room was so quiet I heard the boy's soft footsteps as he wandered in from the back. Just beyond the windows, like a sound shadow, I sensed the restless murmur of the sea.

There were four of them — three more than necessary to take a small woman into custody. Especially a woman as small as me. Despite having eaten better in the previous six years than in my entire life, Selina often grumbled that I still looked like a child.

My *djellaba*, a deep maroon robe with lavender blossoms embroidered on the sleeves, rustled dryly, despite my attempts to remain still. Though I rarely wore a scarf when the tearoom had no customers, early that morning I had combed my hair back and wrapped my head in a soft mauve cloth. Headscarves are meant to signal a woman's modesty before both men and god, but I've always found that they draw one's gaze to a woman's face. I didn't want anyone to look at my face — at least, not until I had prepared the face that would best protect me.

They were dressed in full uniform: blue shirts so dark they might have been black, and red berets set at a hard angle over the left eye. Their shoulders were trimmed in gold braid, and each wore bright slashes of color pinned over his heart. Later, Hania would explain that those slashes signaled their rank in the Casablanca police force. To me, it seemed those little banners hid away their hearts, making it easier to follow whatever orders they were given.

When the glass doors opened I thought first of their boots, which sent a spray of fine sand across the white tiles. The boy, suddenly afraid, buried his face in my skirt. Whispering his name, I lifted him into my arms.

The look in the eyes of the man who stepped forward, peeling black glasses from his face, made it clear they would tolerate no resistance.

"Are you Senhaji Rana, who sometimes calls herself Hajar?"

Gently shifting the child to my good hip, I answered with utmost courtesy: "I am al-Maghribi Zahra Leila."

For the briefest moment he paused, eyes wandering over the few visible strands of my henna-reddened hair, thick-scarred cheek and my too-bright, apple green eyes. My mother's eyes.

A whisper of something like desire passed through his gaze, a whisper I'd seen in the face of every man who'd had complete power over me. My heart sped up, and for the first time in years, my hands grew wet with fear.

"Were you once known as either Raja, or Hajar, the servant of Yusef Hakim Senhaji?" he repeated, testily.

Now I paused. There was no use in lying, for my scar, clearly visible despite the make-up I wore to civilize my face, was the brand of my past. I also knew that to argue might bring disaster not only to me, but also to the blame-less people I loved.

Yet to offer no resistance would dishonor the liberty I'd fought so hard to possess. So I struggled to look into his eyes.

"Yes. I am this person."

"Then you will come with us."

I heard a gasp behind me. Aliah, her hands covered with dough, had appeared beside Shada in the workroom door.

"Leila?" Aliah whispered, looking from the policeman to me.

Turning slowly, I set the boy on the floor. He scurried across the room to Aliah and leaned against her thighs.

"Leila?" she repeated, the word drawn out. "What do they want?"

A young man with black eyes and deeply pocked skin, spoke up. "Madame, please raise your arms. I must search you."

I turned my face away as he felt my arms, shoulders, waist and upper thighs through my *djellaba*.

"Leila?" Aliah repeated, "I don't understand."

"We are here to take your friend for a talk," the young man answered. He stepped back and nodded to his superior.

"Why are you doing this?" Aliah asked, with the cour-age of a woman who had never been in police custody. "I assure you she's done nothing wrong."

"That's not for you to decide," he replied.

"But certainly —"

"Aliah," I interrupted softly as I arranged my scarf to cover the curls that had escaped, "please call Walid. He will know what to do. Hania will be here soon to pick up the boys. I would prefer you don't tell Selina just yet. She'll worry."

Carefully I closed the top clasp of my *djellaba*, aware of the officers' seeking eyes. "Finish the baking exactly as you do every night," I said to Shada's bewildered silence. Speaking calmly to hide my trembling voice, I added, "Lock up as usual. I'll be back tomorrow, god willing."

Both women stared as I bent to reach for the small cosmetic bag from a cabinet at my feet. The bag, holding a comb, soap, underwear, a hand towel and toothbrush, had been packed for many months.

After all, this moment was no surprise.

Our footfalls seemed to echo as I crossed the floor, surrounded by the men, and entered the mounting twilight. Three little boys kicked a ball on the beach below the seawall, and the hollow crack of leather on stone, amid the rough music of their shouts, sent a flock of seagulls screaming into the sky. A woman sitting on a bench nearby hushed her restless baby with a quiet song, while the small, rat-faced dog barked shrilly from a balcony across the street. The world smelled of asphalt, exhaust, cardamom, and the foaming, turquoise sea.

Strangely, as we walked toward the vehicle, I felt a part of each and every living creature around me. I also seemed to be a thousand miles away, watching myself, and my uniformed escorts, from the distance of the cloudless sky. Most of all, I felt something close to relief.

My years of waiting were finally at an end.

Now I was liberated from my freedom.

I was, once again, a slave.

1.   GHOSTS

2010

I knew Hania was unhappy by the scent of salt in the bread.

When her husband Rachid was satisfied with the couscous and little Tariq had slept through the night, the dough rose evenly and sweetly in the pre-dawn light. This morning, however, the batter clung to the rolling pin and Hania cursed when instead of a pinch, a palmful of salt slipped between her fingers and into the flour.

After three years in the bakery's small workroom, I knew the dance of Hania's hands as she molded the loaves, the way the fine hairs along her forehead curled in the bursts of damp heat from the open oven door, and how the smell of baking bread revealed the depths of her mood.

I also knew when it was best not to speak.

"Sometimes I think I married too soon," she grumbled as she closed the oven. "I already have one son, and another baby on the way, and Rachid goes on and on about how little money he makes."

Crossing the room, she lifted Tariq from his high chair, set him on her hip and handed him a sweet roll, which he chewed happily.

"Some days Rachid says I should work in an office, or teach. But who would allow me to bring the new baby to work? And how would you and mother manage without me?"

Nodding in agreement, I drew a mixing spoon through a bowl of batter. Though no longer fearful when alone with her, I was, nonetheless, aware that Hania angered quickly when interrupted.

"Other days, Rachid complains that being here keeps me from cleaning our apartment properly. Of course, he doesn't complain that because of this bakery he can watch football on his own wide-screen television, instead of going to his brother's. He bought a computer last year with the money I earned, and now he's talking about a new car. He forgets that to house a camel, you must make the doors higher!"

Hania peered at her son as if seeking traces of his father. "I know Rachid only wants a better life for us," she added, shaking her head slowly, "but sometimes —"

Suddenly she broke off. "Leila, you must look at me when I'm talking to you!"

Setting down my spoon obediently, I glanced up. "I'm looking at you, Hania."

"No, you're not. You're looking *through* me."

"I'm sorry," I replied.

"No excuses! You must learn to raise your eyes!"

Taking a deep breath, I wiped my hands on my apron and looked directly into Hania's face.

Our eyes met and held. Something shifted in her expression and the room seemed colder, as if the sun had moved behind a cloud. Her gaze fell to her son's dark curls and she drew him closer.

"Leila," she murmured, "it's I who should apologize. Sometimes I forget what you've been through —"

"I'm glad you forget," I assured her. "When you forget, I forget for a little while, too."

Returning to my work, I added soft butter and honey to the batter, then dusted it with lemon peel.

Hania placed Tariq on the floor, and he skipped joyfully toward me. I set my bowl aside and pulled him to my knees as his mother walked to the sink, smoothed her apron over her belly, and began wiping down the counter.

Footsteps descended from the apartment above, and Hania's older brother, Walid, walked in. Tall and pensive, Walid was a man of few words. He shared his mother's brown curls and perceptive eyes, but his face remained locked behind a wall of sorrow.

Greeting us politely, Walid removed the keys from the hook by the door and vanished into the alley. Moments later, the delivery truck growled awake and lumbered into the dawn.

Hania gave me a measuring glance, so I busied myself by wiping crumbs from her son's mouth. Though always respectful, Walid was kind to me in the way one is kind to a child. This did not displease me, for I had known only pain when men saw me as a woman.

Still avoiding Hania's gaze, I smoothed the curls from Tariq's dark eyes, and pressed my lips against his alabaster forehead.

"Leila —" she asked, her voice now filled with design, "don't you ever dream of a different life?"

"No, Hania. I'm happy here."

"Your idea of happiness is being trapped from dawn until dark in this small room!"

I chose to say nothing and hoped she would do the same. For several minutes the kitchen was silent, which was a gift, for Hania rarely conquered her need to speak.

Now I, in turn, watched as she moved to the oven. Her thick braid, hennaed the deep auburn of the horizon sunset, swung nearly to her waist. My hair was cut short and pinned back from my face. A woman's hair is said to be part of her beauty. I wanted no one to find me beautiful.

Only in the kitchen — and only when Walid had left for the day — did I dare remove my robes and expose the thatch of scars on my shoulders, back, and chest. These wounds had been hewn into my skin three years before, when a servant beat me with a cane. The beating also crushed the bridge of my nose, and shattered my left cheek like broken stone.

Rocking little Tariq in my arms, I hummed the song that reminded me most of my mother. Hania and Walid's mother, Selina, was singing it the day I'd wandered — filthy, frightened, and starving — into the open door of their bakery. I hadn't heard the song for many years — not since the night my father gave me to three men as payment for his debts.

I was twelve years old.

Tariq now nestled his head against my shoulder, tiny thumb in his mouth. Hania leaned back, stretched, and pressed her palms into the small of her back.

"You should wear brighter colors," she remarked, losing her battle with silence. "No one notices a woman in gray."

"I don't want to be noticed, Hania."

"Then how will you find a husband?"

"I don't want a husband."

"Every woman wants a husband! You're standing in the shadow of your own sun, Leila. You've got to stop hiding."

"I have good reason to hide."

"It's been three years. Do you think they're still searching for a servant?"

"I was their possession, and such men don't share their possessions with others."

"Well, what about your 'Young Master's' wife? Wouldn't she try to stop them?"

"I doubt it," I answered, picturing Young Mistress' face.

Hania raised her brows. Again stroking her
leaned with sudden weariness against the edge of

"The most important thing is that you got
believe, even if you don't, that your happiness is worth
seeking."

"Those who leave home in search of happiness pursue a
shadow," I said. "Here, I have everything I need."

"That," Hania replied, "is because they taught you to
need nothing."

Tariq slid off my lap and skipped back to his mother.
Hania bent to hug him.

"You're very like my brother, Leila. He lives so completely in the past that he has no future."

"Perhaps memory is his best companion," I replied
quietly.

Despite Hania's words, I knew I would never live like other
women: my scarred face remained grotesque, despite Hania's
best efforts with makeup. A beating by my Young Master left
me walking like a much older woman. And, as Hania so often
complained, I still struggled to meet anyone's eyes.

"Leila," Hania called. Hesitantly I looked up. "I know
I pester you too much, but you can't spend your life haunted by your past. You deserve some joy in this world."

"I'm at peace," I answered. "Peace is a far greater gift
than anything I could hope for."

Still, some nights I lay awake. Light from the street
formed humped shadows that mounted the walls like
the feral dogs lurking in the passageways below.

My thoughts often turned to my father's lurching figure, rising against the glow of embers in our mountain hut. Tensing,

I recalled his bitter odor of wine and sweat as he reached for my mother. It was her determined silence that I'd called upon when Young Master threw himself on top of me, wrenching up my robes and pinning my arms to the floor.

Other nights, I willed my mind back to the sea-scented breezes of Essaouira, the city where I'd been held captive. What had become of the young man and woman who took me away to Casablanca? Where were they today? Did they even remember me?

Hania often spoke of perfect love between a man and a woman. Perhaps it existed for others, but I had glimpsed it only once — on that day, between two people I would never see again.

Fatih Mouharam fell in March that year, and the streets of the *souk* were swept clean and hung with fluttering red and green banners. As had become my reluctant custom, I agreed to go out with Hania, her husband Rachid, and Walid — but only after nightfall.

Hania insisted I wear a new, cornflower-blue *djellaba* and cover my hair with a matching headscarf. I rarely wore such bright colors, and feared the eyes of the entire city would find me.

"Nonsense," she repeated as she traced my lids with a fine shadow of kohl, and shaped my brows. "Everyone will be enjoying themselves, not thinking about you. And here," she added as she handed me a tiny vial, "I want you to use this." When I opened my mouth to refuse, she closed her fingers tightly over mine. "There's nothing wrong with wearing perfume, Leila. It's one of the pleasures of being a woman."

"It's not necessary," I protested.

"Stop complaining. You live in the city now, even if you and my mother never stop talking about your precious mountains!"

"Hania —"

"—You'll feel better about yourself when you look your best. I want you to walk with your head up and join in the conversation tonight. And remember: no one is going to recognize you! Even if those fools from Essaouira were in Casablanca — and they're *not* — they'd be looking for the scarecrow who turned up at Mother's door three years ago, not the pretty girl in these lovely new clothes."

Soon I found myself enveloped in a cloud of Egyptian sandalwood as I walked, at a pace slow enough to avoid hurting my hip, beside her. Hania excitedly described a shawl she planned to purchase as a birthday gift for Selina. Rachid strolled along with Walid, a few steps ahead. I could hear Rachid reciting the prices of the cars parked along the boulevard. He said the best cars came from Germany, and that one day he would certainly own one. Walid listened politely, saying nothing.

Crowds poured into Mohammed V Square, gathering in circles around men playing *ouds* and *bendirs*, and stopping to purchase grilled meat and fresh fruit juice from the many food stands. The noise was so loud Hania grasped my hand and brought her face close to mine, so I could hear her speak.

"You see, Leila? You have no reason to worry. No one's paying any attention to us at all." This was untrue, for even though Hania was clearly a married woman with her husband walking just a few paces ahead, many eyes swept her burgundy *djellaba*, gold-threaded headscarf and bright, handsome face.

Slowly we made our way through the crowds and onto the causeway built above the sea. Unmarried couples strolled side-by-side, not daring to touch, their family members close behind; young parents pushed sleeping babies in their carriages, for it was far past bedtime. As always, my thoughts were drawn to the water, barely visible in the night, yet murmuring its deep-throated lullaby.

Many old houses, once part of the ancient city walls, were being torn down and replaced with tall, glass-fronted structures. Rachid pointed out a new building under construction on the waterfront, just meters from the shore. The men stopped walking as we drew alongside it. Hania and I stopped, too, and sank down on a bench facing the beach. Lounge chairs and umbrellas stood stacked against the wall beneath us.

"I'm trying to convince Rachid to name the baby Idriss, after my father, if it's a boy," Hania explained as she stroked the curve of her robe. "If it's a girl, I'm thinking of Amina. Of course, Rachid prefers Mohammed for a boy and Rachida for a girl. I don't mind, as long as —"

I let my thoughts drift to the waves that sewed their tapestry of whispered rhythm on the sand. Sometimes I wondered that the waves never stopped their rushing journey to the shore, like the great, swelling heartbeat of the world. That heartbeat had been my guide through many years of sorrow, until the day it led me to —

"Leila!" Hania tugged my hand, worry in her eyes. "What's wrong?"

Looking up, I found Rachid and Walid also staring at me.

"I — I'm sorry. I was listening to the water."

"Listening to the water?" Hania repeated, annoyed. "Listen to *this*, instead!" She pointed to a large sign, written in both Arabic and another language I took to be French.

"*Spacious suites on the ground floor available for rent. Retail and food services welcome. Oceanfront and street front locations possible. Address all inquiries to the site manager.*"

She turned back to me. "Wouldn't it be wonderful to work here, right next to the beach? Imagine having an office facing the water. Or perhaps a very elegant boutique with the latest fashions from Paris! Of course, it's so beautiful we'd get nothing done!"

"It would be perfect for a bakery," I murmured. "A bakery with a bright tearoom and walls of windows. People could sit there all day, or come in from the beach to eat something sweet and rest for a while."

As if surprised to hear me speak, Walid stared at me a moment longer before glancing back at the water.

"That's true," he agreed. "A bakery in this location could do quite well."

"But the rent would be mountain high!" Rachid exclaimed. "Even if you worked day and night, you'd never sell enough bread to succeed!"

"A good tourist season might cover the rest of year," Walid mused.

"Perhaps if everything was overpriced," Rachid argued, "but then your *only* customers would be tourists."

"The bakery could serve our people, too," I said hesitantly, knowing it was unwise to disagree with Hania's husband. "The tourists will want the food they eat at home. But we could also sell bread at regular prices for those who live in the quarter."

"And when the weather is cold," Hania added, "women could spend their afternoons in our tearoom overlooking the sea!"

Rachid shook his head. "Few Moroccans have time and money to waste that way."

"But our people do frequent cafes," Walid began, "and—"

"— Most buy their bread from bakeries," I added bravely.

"That's right!" Hania exclaimed, agreeing with her brother and me.

"You could never raise enough capital to open a business here," Rachid replied.

Walid shrugged. "The government always says it will support new ventures."

Rachid barked out a laugh. "The government says many things. We shouldn't be stupid enough to believe them."

"Still, it might be worth looking into."

"Are you mad? This is not for people like us!"

"Because we're Berber?"

"Of course, Walid! The government won't even let us name our children after our forefathers."

"We pay taxes like everyone else," Walid said. "If we want to open a business, we should try to do it."

"A handful of bees is worth a sack full of flies. You already have your mother's deliveries in the mornings, and an office job during the day. Don't you think that's enough?"

"A bakery on the waterfront could give us a very different life."

"What about your mother's business?"

Walid fell silent for a moment. "We'd probably have to give the old bakery up," he conceded.

"And Mother would never agree to that," Hania said.

"That's right," Rachid agreed. "Besides, running a small bakery in the *souk* is one thing. Operating a business like this, on the waterfront, would be entirely different. You'd need special licenses, permits, and face it: if a rich man steals it's a 'mistake,' but if a poor man makes a mistake, he has *stolen!*"

"Still," Walid said, "other people manage to do it."

"Those people have money and friends in the government. Even if you could find the right people to pay off, soon someone would decide they wanted a piece of your profit. And if your new business failed, the bank would take your mother's bakery, too."

Walid was silent.

"And think about your mother," Rachid continued. "I know she can manage the bakery in the *souk*, but do you really think she could handle something this big?"

"I would help —" Hania began, but was silenced by her husband's piercing stare.

"You have enough to do in your own home," he said to her. "It's already difficult when you spend so much time at your mother's. And how do you expect to continue in the bakery once the baby is born?"

I stole a glance at Hania, who opened her mouth, but closed it without speaking.

"And one other thing," Rachid added, still looking pointedly at his wife. "I wouldn't want you working around tourists unless Walid or I was present."

Hania rolled her eyes. "Nothing would happen, Rachid."

"That's correct," he replied firmly, "because I wouldn't allow you to work there unless a male family member was with you."

Walid considered his brother-in-law. Rachid instantly read his face.

"Come now, Walid. If you sleep in a swamp, you wake up with snakes. You know these Frenchmen have little respect for our women. Leaving your mother and sister alone with the tourists would invite a scandal, and we certainly couldn't hire a stranger to be with them all day. One of us would have to leave his job and work in the bakery. You studied far too long to give up your career!"

"That's true," Walid conceded, and I heard an odd dullness, which I recognized as defeat, enter his voice.

Rachid clapped him on the shoulder. "Face it, my brother: if you want to buy a Mercedes Benz, you won't do it by selling *eclairs*!" He burst into brittle laughter that echoed against the buildings across the street.

Walid turned away, his face closing.

"Leila, look at that dog!" Hania said in a falsely cheerful voice. She pointed to a large woman in a silvery *kaftan* on a balcony across the street. The woman, holding a small, long-haired, rat-faced dog in her arms, shouted at a young man below. The dog barked shrilly, its entire body shaking with the effort. The yelps caused the woman to yell even louder, and the dog, in turn, sent up a high-pitched, screeching howl.

Hania began to laugh and, after a moment, Rachid joined in, too. Even I laughed a little. Hania took my arm, and ignoring Walid's thoughtful silence, we walked on, the glass building, like so many dreams, already behind us.

Several weeks later Walid's feet on the stairs marked the end of my evening prayers. Selina had gone into the bath, so I hurried to put away my prayer rug and return to my room.

As I closed my door he called my name softly.

"Leila, I apologize for the late hour, but may I speak to you for a moment?"

Reluctant to be alone with Walid, especially at night, I slipped on my *kaftan*, walked into the small clean kitchen and stood at the door, gaze fixed on the table. Walid set his shoulder bag on the floor and poured a glass of tea from the samovar. He sank into a chair, sipped from the steaming glass and set it down carefully.

"Leila, are you happy here?"

I peered up, on guard. Though clearly tired from his workday, Walid's green eyes seemed unusually bright.

"I — I thank you again for allowing me to live in your home," I responded cautiously.

"Please don't thank me. My mother is delighted you've chosen to stay with us. Still, I wonder how you feel. You say so little — at least, when I'm present."

"I'm sorry." Again, I fixed my gaze on the table.

"I don't want you to apologize."

Hesitating, I now concentrated on hiding my trembling hands in my robes. "Please tell me what you'd like to hear."

"I'd like to hear more about what you were thinking on *Fatih Mouharam.*"

"Pardon?"

"I'd like to hear your thoughts about opening a tearoom in that new building on the beach."

My eyes widened, though I tried to keep my face blank. This was either a trick or a mistake. Why would Walid ask my opinion about a fantasy?

"This may sound strange," he continued, as if reading my mind, "but since that night on the beach I have thought of little else."

"But after what Rachid said —"

"Rachid is a fool who loves the sound of his own voice. Though he is a good enough husband to my sister, he wants whatever he sees on television. He can't tell us how to live our lives."

Walid calmly raised the glass to his lips, but the fingers of his other hand tapped the table in a quick, quiet rhythm.

"Leila, I've gone back to look at the building site several times. I called the management company a few days ago to ask about renting the ground floor."

He paused, waiting for my reaction. The only sound was the nervous drumming of his fingers. After a few moments he continued speaking, as if to fill the silence.

"It is indeed quite expensive, but the government is offering special loans for new businesses. The process is relatively simple. The true difficulty lies in getting signatures from the proper authorities. My friend's cousin, who is an attorney, has agreed to help me with that. However," he looked into my face, "I'll need your help in convincing Mother."

"Convincing her —?" I stammered.

"— To open the tearoom on the beach. We'll have to use this bakery as collateral."

He noted my confused expression. "This means the government will hold the deed to this bakery until we've paid off the loan for the new business."

I remained mute, fearful of an improper response. Walid again sipped his tea, grimaced, then dropped a sugar cube into the glass and swirled it absently.

Finally I spoke. "You are certain about this?"

For a moment I thought he might become angry. Instead, sadness darkened his eyes.

"Leila, courage is nothing more than fear that has said its prayers. We could go on living here in the souk, working our hearts out, earning a few *dinars* every day and hoping our lives will improve."

"We are very blessed," I murmured.

"Yes," he agreed. "But my father sent Hania and me to school, even when he needed our help in the bakery, so we could have a better life than his. He used to say that dawn comes only once to wake us. I think he would have approved of this plan."

I looked away, picturing the tearoom in my mind. I had dreamed of few things in my life — to be a shopkeeper's wife when just a girl, to see my mother's face once again, and to walk each day beside the water.

Glancing back, I found Walid looking directly into my face.

"It would be very difficult," I whispered.

"Yes," he agreed.

"We'd have to work very hard."

"This is true."

"People might not come at first."

"That is possible."

"And we'd have to bake new things — things the tourists will buy."

"I agree."

"I don't know how to make French pastries."

"We'll find someone who does."

"And Hania's husband is correct: a man must be there."

"I would be there."

"You would—"

"Yes." Gently Walid set his glass on the table. "Father often said that the heart, not money, is the strength of the merchant. I'd be happy to leave my job and instead work in our tearoom by the sea."

Though my heart leapt at his words, I couldn't look away from the sugar swirling at the bottom of his glass.

He followed my gaze. "What is it, Leila?"

"You must allow me to remain in the kitchen."

"No one will hurt you."

"I don't wish to be seen."

"Leila, fear is a cancer. You must fight, or it will consume you."

"Please," I said.

Walid was silent a long moment, before nodding gravely. "I will respect your wish, my sister."

"And I will do everything I can," I replied, glancing up, "for your tearoom by the sea."

His somber face brightened. "The biggest challenge will be convincing Mother. After so many years, she won't want to close this bakery."

"It's not my place to speak of such things."

"My mother considers you her daughter."

"Oh, no. Hania —"

"Hania thinks of you as her sister."

"Still, I have no right —"

"Leila, your hard work has made my mother's bakery one of the most successful in the *souk*. You have every right."

"It wasn't my work alone."

"The kite only flies because of its tail. You do the work of three people and ask for nothing in return!"

"But you all give me so much —"

"We could never give you half as much as you've given us."

His words made my heart do a little dance. I peered hard at him, looking for any hint of mockery.

"Leila," he said, "when you take the right path, even thorns can't hurt you."

Walid stood, and I took a nervous step back. He ignored this, though I'm sure he saw it.

"Thank you," he said in a low voice, "for speaking with me. I sometimes go for weeks without hearing your voice."

"I didn't realize you wanted me to speak," I replied, honestly.

"I know," he answered sadly. "I know."

Though I spent the entire week repeating Walid's words in my mind, each time I was alone with Selina I was unsure what to say. Then, one evening, after the final customer purchased our last two baguettes, she came to me in the workroom and sat beside me at the table.

"Little rose petal," she began, using the nickname she'd given me, "my son has come to me with an idea. Walid wants to close this bakery and open a tearoom in a new building on the beach beside the sea. He says we'll borrow money from the bank to do this."

Her green eyes, identical to her son's, flickered around the room. "I have worked in these rooms for over thirty years — since my beloved husband brought me to Casablanca as a bride. My children were born in the apartment upstairs and played right here, beneath this table, while I baked the bread that fed my family and neighbors. This has been my life.

"Leila, our business is thriving. Many people come from across the *souk* to buy your breads and pastries. I don't like to disagree with my son. He believes he's doing what's best, but I don't understand why we need to take such a risk. Do you think Walid is right?"

"I hardly know, Mother."

Selina paused, tilting her head to the side. "It is often said that a wise woman has much to say, but chooses to be silent. I know silence has been your sister for much of your life. But I ask you, now, to speak. I truly wish to hear your thoughts."

Hesitating, I recalled my mother's warning that in deep water it was wisest not to open one's mouth. I feared my words might anger her, or cause Walid to turn against me. Though I believed Selina would never deliberately cause me harm, I knew well what a man — even a man as quiet as Walid — might do.

Above all, I feared being sent back to the streets, where I doubted I would long survive.

But Selina deserved the truth.

"It was I who first spoke of opening a tearoom on the beach," I admitted. "It was only a daydream. I never thought anyone would take it seriously."

I placed my hands flat on the worktable and contemplated my scars.

"I know nothing of contracts, or banks, or how to start a business. But if you and Walid decide to open this tearoom by the sea, I will work as hard as I can to make our guests welcome, so they'll be happy to return. In this way I can thank you for everything you've given me.

"And," I added, whispering the words we both knew, but found nearly impossible to say, "in this tearoom I think your son might find a new life."

2. SHADOW DANCE

2011

I'd never have guessed that Selina would fall so deeply in love with the idea of the tearoom by the sea. The project brought new life between Selina and Walid, who now spent many evenings in the little apartment above the bakery. Selina's joy at his presence echoed throughout the house in her constant laughter and glorious, trilling songs.

Each evening Walid sat with us, making lists of everything we'd need to purchase, from larger ovens to bud vases. I'd never seen him so focused on anything except his studies, and to my surprise, he always included me in the discussions.

"Should we begin by selling bread, or concentrate on pastries when we first open the tearoom?"

Hesitant to reply, I glanced at Selina.

"Leila?" she prodded.

"We should do both, though since many customers will be tourists, I think our pastries will be more popular."

"I'll ask my friend Amin whether he's got a good French pastry book in his bookstore," Walid replied, adding to his list.

"I can't read French," I reminded him.

"No matter," he answered with a smile. "You and Mother will sing the pastries to perfection!"

Selina burst into laughter. "You should join us! We'll turn you into a baker, too!"

"I might poison half the city."

"Ah, my practical son! Always thinking about losing customers!"

"Well, we do need one or two."

"Don't worry, *habib* — our tearoom will be the most celebrated in all of Casablanca!"

"Perhaps we could sell *shawarma* or *falafel* at a window on the street," he said, returning to his list.

"Certainly," Selina agreed.

"We could have an ice cream machine," I suggested.

"Absolutely," he replied, making another note.

"And we'd better start looking for additional help. If we're not careful," Selina said, winking at me, "Leila won't stop working, even to sleep."

Walid glanced up. "Well, Leila, is my mother right?"

I looked at Selina, then back at her son. "We must move the earth before we smell the flowers."

"You're right," Selina agreed, placing her arm around my shoulders. "We're lucky you're here, my daughter."

Despite many delays in obtaining a loan, the required licenses, and completing the construction, we opened *Chez Selina* nine months after we first came upon the building. With a kitchen large enough to hold five ovens, a rotisserie, and a cold storage room, we were able to offer fresh bread, gyros sandwiches and both French and Moroccan pastries to our guests throughout the day.

Three walls of windows welcomed glorious light as the sun migrated the horizon from dawn to dusk. Tables topped with white marble reflected the pale morning, golden noon and saffron evening, all set against the pure white sand and impossibly blue-green water.

Glass cases next to the kitchen doors permitted us to quickly restock the bread and pastries that seemed to vanish as quickly as we could bake them. Walid sold warm sandwiches and ice cream through an open window at the street, and the scents of honey, sugar, warm butter, and cinnamon beckoned the neighborhood to our door.

Hania insisted on helping with the baking in the early mornings, despite having given birth to Idir, her second son. In the lavender hours before sunrise, Selina, Hania, and I prepared many trays of Moroccan and French pastries — and some three hundred loaves of bread, to sell throughout the day. Though at first it was difficult to rise even earlier, we all knew gold lives in the mouth of the morning.

Selina hired Aliah, a short, round-faced woman who worked to support herself and her daughter after her husband abandoned them, and Shada, a quiet girl whose mother insisted she pay rent if she refused to marry. Selina handled customers in the tearoom, while Aliah, who had worked at a French bakery, assisted with the *eclaires, milles feuilles, religeuses,* and *palmiers* the French tourists loved. Neither woman asked why I rarely left the kitchen, nor why my face was so badly scarred. Indeed, they seemed to understand that at some point I had displeased a man.

Selina was, of course, the heart of her tearoom: fretting babies ceased to cry when she smiled into their eyes, and mothers stared with happy confusion when Selina made them giggle. She sent students to the quietest corners, and their glasses of mint tea were refilled without question. Young lovers sometimes stole in, peering over their shoulders for watchful parents or siblings, and Selina gently reminded them to be respectful of their families. Never did I see anyone anger at her words. The magic she conjured in my heart, teaching me to rise with hope every day, seemed to enchant everyone who came into the light of her eyes.

If work is prayer, Walid has assured his place in heaven. Every day he delivered bread to local schools and hospitals, sold gyros to walk-up customers, and managed the stocks of flour, sugar, yeast, salt, butter, milk, eggs, nuts, spices, and other articles for the tearoom. In the evenings he settled the accounts, while Selina and I rested. Though darkness still paced in the shadows of his eyes, he never complained or seemed unhappy.

He gains a double victory who conquers himself.

In the evenings, after returning to our apartment above the old bakery in the *souk*, I sometimes watched television with Selina, though the programs she enjoyed — stories with many characters who fell in and out of love — seemed strange to me. I much preferred to take the books Hania and Walid shared with me, and practice reading, alone in my room. I particularly loved poetry, and read the book written by a poet from the mountains of my birth — a gift from Walid — over and over again.

One evening I heard a quiet knock at my door. Walid spoke from just beyond the threshold. I sat up quickly and adjusted my *kaftan*, though when I opened my door, I found him staring respectfully at the floor.

Dressed in one of the shirts he wore when he worked in an office, he'd cut his hair earlier in the week, so his thick curls framed his forehead like petals. He was also freshly-shaven, though it was late in the evening, and even stranger, he smelled strongly of amber with a faint trace of citron.

"Excuse me, Leila," he said quietly. "I know this is your time to rest, but I wanted to ask a favor."

"Yes?"

"I was planning to go see a film, and my friend just called to say he can't come."

I waited, unsure what he meant.

He waited, too, then cleared his throat. "I thought perhaps, well, if you wouldn't mind giving up your evening, you might agree to see the film with me."

A sudden coolness passed through my body. "A film? In a cinema?"

"Yes. We wouldn't go far. The cinema's near the mosque, just a few streets away."

"Are Hania and Rachid coming, too?"

"No. They're busy with the baby."

"Yes, of course."

An awkward silence followed.

"Well, if you'd prefer to wait until Hania and Rachid can come, we could try some other time."

"I — I've never been to a cinema."

"I see," he said quickly. "You're probably more interested in, well —" his eyes flickered up — "in your books."

The room began to whir. Walid was asking me to go out, into the darkness, and into a room filled with strangers. Selina wouldn't be there. Hania wouldn't be there. I would be alone with a man, in the souk, in a place I'd never been.

Alone in the dark with a man.

What if we were separated? What if he became angry with me for some reason, and left me? What if someone saw me who knew me from my earlier life? What if he tried to touch me?

Walid stood by the door, waiting for my answer. Heart quaking, I tried to frame a refusal polite enough to avoid his anger.

Then, a quiet voice entered my mind.

This is Walid, the voice said. Walid, who helped you learn to write after discovering the truth about your past. Who brought you the book of poetry from your home. Who took you back to your village, hoping to restore you to your mother.

Walid, who listens when you speak.

Walid, who sees your scars, but never looks away.

He began to close the door. "Perhaps another time. I'm sorry I disturbed you."

"Wait!" I called out, surprising us both. "I'll be ready in a moment!"

We walked through the evening streets, now quiet and smelling strongly of the bleach the merchants used to clean their stands, and the sidewalks outside their businesses. The iron grills on the stores were closed, and voices drifted from the open windows above.

I smelled the rich, heady scent of roasting lamb from one window, the cumin in a vegetable *tajine* from another. Television sets sent flickering blue lights through lacy curtains, and the lilting voices of *Djudjura*, Hania's favorite singers, spilled from a doorway.

Walid's head seemed to flick up at the sound of children's laughter around a corner just ahead of us, and I again sensed how much he still mourned his wife and infant son, who would now have been six years old.

The cinema was a large, humid room filled with cushioned seats that faced a very large white wall resembling stretched cotton. The air was heavy with the scents of smoke, fried potatoes, and sweat. Many people, carrying bottles of juice and bags of nuts, had already taken their seats. A sign outside the door said smoking was not allowed in the theater, so men in blue jackets walked along the aisles with flashlights, checking for the glow of cigarettes.

Walid purchased a small bag of pistachios and led me to seats near the rear, just as the film started. Though I loved the sweet, soft meat inside the reddened shells, I forgot all about the pistachios he'd poured into my palms when the screen suddenly burst into life. I was speechless at the size of the faces, the speed of the cars, and noise they made as they roared through the streets of a place called Los Angeles.

For nearly two hours I stared at these images, understanding little, but shocked at the wild clothing and colorful make-up of the women, the castle-like houses, and intense colors of the grass and trees. I was also struck by the strange cruelty of the men in the film, who used guns to shoot other men for no reason at all.

When it ended we filed out with the noisy crowd, and Walid led me to a quiet table at the rear of a café terrace across the street. He ordered tea, then sat beside me in the shadows, eating the last of the nuts and watching the people entering the theater.

"Well, what did you think of your first movie?" he asked when the tea arrived.

"Thank you for asking me to come," I answered. "It was truly wonderful."

He smiled, his face seeming unused to the task. "I'm glad you enjoyed it. But what did you *really* think?"

"Well," I began, unsure if he would be offended if I told the truth. "I didn't understand why everyone was so — so angry. They seemed to be very rich, yet they fought all the time. And," I paused, "— why did they all try to kill each other?"

Walid laughed out loud, then shook his head. "I don't know, Leila. I've seen many of these movies from America, and they all seem to center around people committing murder. It's strange that those who have so much seem to enjoy causing pain and death."

"Perhaps they have so much, they live in constant fear of losing it."

"Yes," he said in agreement. "My father used to say that the fewer one's desires, the happier one's life."

I sat very still, unsure what to do next. Walid took a sip of tea and his gaze wandered over the square. The front of the cinema was empty and the little booth where tickets were sold was dark. Walid's thoughts seemed far away, and his smile faded. I imagined he was thinking of other films, perhaps films he'd seen with Nora, his late wife.

Suddenly I understood that during the years I was trapped inside the house above the sea, struggling to survive, other people, *normal* people, were living normal lives.

Could I live such a life?

Quietly, almost without meaning to, I said his name. Surprised, Walid peered over his glass at me, eyes focusing on my face. And, though it was difficult, I managed not to lower my gaze.

"Please Walid," I said, "would you tell me about some other films you've seen?"

His face opened. "What would you prefer, Leila? Tales of monsters, or mystery, or perhaps a real Hollywood romance?"

"I know nothing about any of those things," I answered, allowing myself a faint smile, "so they'll all be interesting to me."

"That makes things much easier," he laughed. He then began to speak of movies he loved as a boy, as a young man, and as a husband. He talked about a film in which a giant fish killed swimmers and nearly ate a boat; a movie about soldiers who escaped from a prison camp by digging a tunnel that went on for miles, and a man who jumped over the enemy's wire fences with a motorcycle; and the story of a man and a woman who fell in love, decided to part, then arranged to meet one year later in the tallest building in New York. As I listened, his voice soothed the bird perched on the edge of uncertainty, deep inside my soul.

I suddenly noticed Walid had stopped speaking. I was, without realizing it, staring into his face. I started and quickly looked at my hands, clasped tightly in my lap.

"And now it's your turn," he said.

"What?"

"It's your turn to tell me a story."

"I — I have no stories."

"I'm sure you do. Perhaps you don't think of them as stories."

I asked him what he'd like to hear.

"Tell me about the time when you were happiest."

For a moment my mind whirred. Happy? When had I ever been happy?

But then a memory unthreaded itself from the tangled darkness and drifted forward, frail as a whisper of smoke.

"My father sometimes played a wooden flute, a flute he made with his own hands, and he loved it very much. One night, when I was a very small child, he played for me, and my mother danced."

Walid grew very still. Though my eyes were still cast downward, I felt his gaze on my face.

"We had a house, then, and the night wind, smelling of jasmine, cooled the room where we slept. My father had sold a hide that day, and we had meat and bread soaked in honey for our evening meal."

I closed my eyes tight, as the words seemed to pour from me.

"My mother was very beautiful. Her braid was thick, and long, and fell all the way to her waist. When she stood up to dance, her bracelets sounded like tiny bells, and the threads of her scarf glowed in the firelight."

Though I could scarcely breathe, I could not stop speaking.

"She had green eyes — apple-green eyes, he sometimes said. When she danced, she closed her eyes, and her body grew light, as if she could fly. She smiled at me and said her shadow was her partner. She began to sing as she danced, and her voice, like the night wind, floated on the clouds of the melody. I know I was happy, because that night she was happy."

I reached up to smooth the sudden wetness from my scar.

For some time Walid did not speak.

And, of course, neither did I.

Then I was in a windowless room in the judge's house, lying damp with sweat on my bed. The bell rang in the kitchen, calling me to work, and I scrambled up from my pallet. Exhausted, but frightened, I knew I would not move quickly enough to please the Judge, his blind mother, Hassan or Young Master.

When I tried to rise, however, I found I was bound to the bed by heavy ropes tied around my wrists and ankles.

The more I struggled, the more the ropes tightened on my limbs. I could hear Hassan's voice as he shouted my name, becoming angrier as he drew near. Terror mounting, I tore at the skin on my arms and legs, feeling the rope burn into my flesh.

Suddenly the door banged open and Young Master appeared, eyes black with rage. Slamming the door behind him, he walked, smiling, to the bed, with Hassan's cane over his shoulder. "Stupid, lazy cow," he intoned, pulling my clothes away, even as I struggled against the ropes. "You will pay for making my grandmother wait for you!" He raised the cane and brought it down on my bare breasts.

And I screamed.

Selina was then beside me, curls loose about her shoulders and *kaftan* unzipped. She wrapped her arms around me and, calling my name over and over, rocked me back and forth, back and forth. When I was calm enough to open my eyes I realized that Walid was standing just outside the door, his face in the shadows.

"Little rose petal," Selina murmured, "you're safe here. No one will harm you. Please don't be afraid."

I pressed my tear-stained face against her chest. "I'm so ashamed, mother. Why does it never end?"

"Have faith, child, and you will know peace," she answered in a low voice, so low I was certain Walid couldn't hear. "I think your dreams help release your fear."

"I'm so sorry I woke you," I replied, wiping my eyes.

"Clothes and food are easy to give. What's difficult is to find medicine to heal the soul."

Several mornings later Walid appeared at the back door of the tearoom, where Hania and I were baking.

"You're still here?" his sister remarked. "You're going to be late with the deliveries."

"I'd like to speak with Leila before I go."

Hania looked at me, then back to her brother. "Why are you being so formal? You can talk to her any time."

Ignoring Hania, he asked if he might sit with me for a few minutes.

Hania laughed out loud. "What's wrong with you, Walid? Why would you ask for permission to come into the kitchen?"

"Leila," he repeated, "might I join you?"

Hania shook her head, carried her tray to the counter and began rolling dough into *croissants*. Walid took her seat at the table and removed a folded paper from his pocket. Turning his body casually toward Hania, he glanced at me only briefly before speaking.

"Leila, you know that neither Shada nor Aliah speak good French, and even though Mother does relatively well, it would help if someone else could assist with the tourists."

"I don't know how to speak French," I said.

"That's why you should consider this." He unfolded the paper and spread it out on the table between us. "The Tourism Council is offering a free French class every Wednesday night from seven to eight-thirty."

Embarrassed, I looked at my hands. "I've never been to school."

"That won't matter. This course is intended for women who come into contact with tourists."

"I can't write very well."

"I'll help you."

"But French is difficult."

"It will, indeed, take time to learn. But you learned to read and write Arabic so quickly, I'm certain you can do it."

I felt myself flush. "I'll seem a fool to the other students."

"They'll be learning, too."

I glanced pleadingly at Hania, who looked from one of us to the other. Surprisingly, she didn't speak.

"I can't go to class at seven. We close at six-thirty and we'd still be cleaning the tearoom."

"I've already spoken to Mother," he replied. "She'll ask Aliah or Shada to stay later on Wednesdays."

I felt tears gather in my eyes. "I don't want to be in the city at night."

"I'll pick you up."

"But the class ends very late."

"It's only an hour later than we usually get home."

"I have to be up by four the next morning —"

"You can start later on Thursdays."

"Hania can't handle the work alone."

"We'll make extra bread the day before."

"We already have so much to do!"

"Mother said you'd refuse," Walid said as he stood, "but I wish you'd consider it."

My hands trembled openly, now. "My place is here, in the kitchen."

"Perhaps, but —"

"I have no desire to leave."

"You have nothing to fear, Leila."

"You promised me I could stay here."

"Leila, I —

"*Leave her alone, Brother!*" Hania's voice rang out.

For some time no one spoke. Walid's green eyes, so much like his mother's, betrayed neither irritation nor impatience.   Instead, I saw only disappointment as he looked from his sister back to me.

"I apologize, Leila."

He ran a restless hand through his hair and walked to the door.

Hania watched him leave, then wiped her palms on her apron and approached the table.   Touching my shoulder gently, she sat down beside me.   She picked up the stone pestle we used to crush almonds, and ran it slowly along the smooth cusp of the bowl.   It made a low, throbbing sound, like the whimper of a mourning dove.

"Leila," she said quietly, "no one will make you go to this class if you really don't want to.   I understand everything you said to my brother.   But, please forgive me — I think there's another reason you're refusing to go."

Our eyes met and I looked away.

"Your parents couldn't read, and no girl in your village went to school.   You were raised to believe it's wrong for women to learn.

"But Leila, *this* is your world, now.   In this world, a woman must be prepared to take care of herself.   Even my mother, who came from a village like yours, understands this."

She picked up the paper and examined it.   "This course is for women who didn't complete an apprenticeship or go to university.   Even though your Arabic is quite good now, learning French will give you the chance for a better future."

"But I don't need French —"

"Perhaps not now, but you never know what the future holds."

Hania put the paper down and grasped my hand.

"I know you're afraid to be out in public, but I believe your fear is unfounded. Even if those people *are* looking for you — and I'm not convinced they are — they'll focus on Marrakech, because it's close to your home, or Agadir, where so many people work in the hotels. There's little chance they'd look for you here, at the other end of the country.

"You're a member of our family, now. You'll stay with us as long as you choose, but you should always prepare for the unexpected. My father used to say that ignorance is the night of the mind. The world is different when you look through the window of learning. And if heaven drops a date, you must open your mouth! Go to the class. You might even enjoy it."

I couldn't tell Hania the thing no one knew, or ever would know: Young Master had used the promise of learning to lure me into a kind of trust, and I'd trusted him until the first time he raped me.

He taught me well: Slaves were not meant to learn.

3.   THE DOVE

Hania was right.   As a girl, I secretly longed for the treasures of the mosque, where the boys of our village vanished every day.   Sometimes I heard their voices chanting verses from the holy book when I crossed the dusty square to seek water from the fountain.   I once asked my mother why girls couldn't go to class and she hushed me, saying such questions were an offense to god.

So I struggled as I left the kitchen that first Wednesday evening and walked with Shada through the busy *souk*. Wrapped in a dark *djellaba*, head down and face hidden, I marked my way back to the tearoom by listening to the merchants haggling with customers, and by absorbing the rose scent of ripe fruit, the blood-iron odor of the meat, and the fading echo of the dying flowers.

The Tourism Council was a building of dark glass, deflecting the chaos of the street with deep, inner calm. Inside, a slender woman in a red leather jacket, a short skirt, and shining, pointed heels, led me in a swirl of gardenia to a room with a large, polished table facing a black wall.

I slid into a chair, my face down.   Soon the other chairs filled with other silent figures.   A woman in a flowered headscarf and knee-length skirt entered the room, strode to the front and said in a bright voice, *"Bonsoir, Mesdames! Commençons tout de suite! Nous avons beaucoups á apprendre!"*

Using a white stick, she made marks on the black wall that she could rub away with a cloth.   I quickly understood that the marks represented sounds, and those sounds had meaning, just as certain sounds formed words in Arabic and Berber.   She asked the class to repeat those sounds again and again, and soon we were laughing at ourselves, and each other, as we struggled to convince our lips and tongues to sound like the teacher. She laughed too, but without cruelty, and we were grateful for her patience.

Still, when the class ended, the women departed quickly, without meeting each other's eyes, and were swallowed by the night. At first I didn't understand why we again became strangers. Then I realized that they, too, were not sure we had the right to be there.

In the weeks that followed, the words I learned slowly began to match those on the French television. As if a light had been turned on, I could understand the stick-thin women and their men, whose hair always seemed too long.

I realized that rather than speaking of great, difficult ideas about life on earth, as I supposed, the people in France talked about the same things our people discussed, though with far less poetry.

Money seemed to be their obsession. Though the actors spoke of food, children's diapers, shining new cars, the soap they used when washing themselves, and even their vacations in our country, the *real* language of French culture was the safety and pleasure that wealth could buy.

No one seemed to work, or at least, not as we understood it. Men in dark suits talked on phones from behind glass desks. Women smoked cigarettes in spacious homes, drove bright cars, and ruffled the curls of charming, golden-haired children.

Everyone drank alcohol before, during and after meals. They went to bed with the husbands and wives of their friends, and sometimes with the spouses of their own brothers and sisters. Though such behavior would have led to honor killings in our culture, the French didn't seem to care much about it at all.

Soon I grew more curious about the tourists who lay, nearly naked, on the beach outside our tearoom. In the afternoons they'd wrap thin cloths around their bodies and sit at our marble-topped tables, drink mint tea, and eat sesame cakes or a *sable nature*. They ignored Selina as she calmed their restless children, then left wads of wet *dinars*, fished from inside their swimsuits, beside plates of half-eaten food.

My curiosity led me, like a tiny mouse, to slip into the tearoom, where I heard the Frenchwomen complain about their dry skin, the challenge of finding a decent wine to drink with dinner, and the lack of good clothing stores in Casablanca.

Often they warned each other that we were thieves, or that all of our men wanted to seduce them. They'd glance across the room at me, faces closing at the sight of my scar.

I asked Walid why the French came to Casablanca if they thought us all lazy fools and thieves.

He laughed. "There are beautiful beaches in the south of France, and we share the same sea, Leila. But the south of France is for the very rich, so those who cannot afford it come to Casablanca."

"But why are they so angry? We make them welcome."

"Yes, but they're reminded they must come to a poor country to feel wealthy."

Selina saved some of the money in a tin box that had once held chocolates given to her by her husband when she was young. At the end of every evening she divided this money between Aliah, Shada and me, also setting a portion aside for Hania. Though we entreated her to keep some for herself, she insisted we were young and deserved the extra pay.

"What would I buy with it?" she'd exclaim. "Everything I need is right here!"

She'd also make me repeat my grammar exercises out loud as we cleaned at night.

"You must learn to speak very well, Leila. Then you can teach me to speak better French, too," she laughed. "Perhaps I can even convince our guests I come from Paris!"

Hania drilled me on the difficult verbs, which seemed to follow no logical pattern. "I never really understood the grammar back in school, so I just memorized it. In the end, the more you talk, the easier it gets."

Walid was, as always, the most patient of my tutors. "It will come in time," he'd say when I struggled with pronunciation. "Even a lamb was born without wool."

Though I'm certain he was pleased, Walid said nothing more than "you're welcome," when I thanked him for suggesting I take the course.

Madame Chafik, my teacher, was studying to be a professor. With a pale Berber complexion and chestnut eyes, she always wore a headscarf secured at her throat by a dove-shaped pin. Because I was afraid to meet her eyes, especially during the first few weeks of class, I spent most of those evenings studying her dove.

Madame smiled often, and burst into tinkling laughter when we said something silly, which made us laugh in turn. "I know this is difficult," she'd say, "but you must remember: knowledge is better than wealth. You must protect your wealth, but knowledge protects you!"

"Leila," she called to me one evening during a break, "might I speak to you for a moment?" The others had scattered, mobile phones in hand, to speak to their families. I lingered in the classroom, having neither a phone, nor anyone to call.

Shyly I approached the table that served as her desk. Our class was held in a conference room used by tourism officials during the day. Posters of the mountains of my birth, the great minaret of Marrakech, and the souk of Casablanca lined the walls. Madame Chafik sat casually on top of the table with her legs crossed at the knee. She always carried a large plastic cup with the words "Sorbonne, Université de Paris," printed on the side.

She had removed her headscarf at the start of class, and her auburn hair shone red in the light. Tiny emerald earrings met my curious gaze. She wore no wedding ring. When standing so close, I could see she was not as young as I believed. Her brown eyes looked tired, yet she smiled.

"I am impressed by how quickly you're making progress!" she said in Arabic.

"Thank you," I replied shyly.

"Where do you come from?"

I gestured toward the portrait of the sunset over the mountain peaks. "I was born in a small village, but left as a child."

"I see," she said, switching to Berber. "Are your parents merchants, here in Casablanca?"

"I do not live with my family."

"Oh — I noticed that a man waits for you after class each week. I assumed he was your brother."

I laughed to hide my embarrassment. "No, Walid is the son of my employer."

She laughed, too. "Clearly you're older than you look! Where do you work?"

"I'm a baker in a tearoom on the beach. It's called '*Chez Selina.*'"

"Yes, I've seen it. What a lovely place to spend your days! Do you use French in your work?"

"I try, but it's difficult."

"You're learning very fast."

"Thank you. My employers help me."

"That's good. It's important to practice." She sipped from her cup and I waited, unsure what to say next.

"Madame, have you — do you go often to Paris?" I asked, forming the sentence carefully in French.

She nodded in approval. "I've been to Paris many times," she answered slowly, to be certain I understood. "My older sister works near Paris, and I used to live with her. I even studied at the Sorbonne one year."

"Really?" I asked, finding it hard to imagine that a woman from our world could attend such a famous university. Seeing my face, she smiled again.

"It's not so special, you know. People from all over the world study in Paris. Perhaps one day you'll study there, too!"

I covered my shy smile, unable to imagine myself there. Madame's perceptive eyes took in my face, scar, calloused hands and simple *djellaba.*

"How many years have you gone to school, Leila?"

I flushed. "I've never had the chance."

"Yet you know how to read and write."

"I've been very blessed."

"I was like you not so long ago," she said. "I grew up on a farm, far from the city. My sister married a man who took her to France, and my father sent me along with her. I had to learn French very fast, and it wasn't easy. That's why I'm studying to be a language professor now. I hope to make it easier for others than it was for me. Though it may be difficult, always remember, Leila: angels bend down their wings to lift up a seeker of knowledge."

By the end of the sixth month I could understand much of what the tourists were saying when I brought fresh pastries into the tearoom. I lingered at the counter, handing the food to Selina even before she translated their requests into Berber. On more than one occasion I greeted French customers who had come in the day before. And when asked to share our recipe for *griouches*, I managed to give detailed instructions, including the complete list of ingredients.

Though I didn't realize it until I saw Selina's smile, I had overcome my fear of learning.

" *B*onsoir, ma soeur," Walid greeted me after class one evening, a few weeks later. I replied in French, proud that I both understood, and could respond in turn.

The night was clear, cool and smelled of wet earth and wood smoke. Though I had grown used to our walks home in the late evenings, I was aware of every sound, every odor, and the shifting light, as we passed beneath the lamps. Carefully I fastened the top buttons of my coat, and tucked the loose ends of my headscarf around my throat.

We threaded our way through the maze of narrow passages, still speaking about what I'd learned in class. Though I tried to hide it, I sometimes struggled to keep up with Walid on the uneven cobblestones, especially on damp nights, when my hip ached. I tripped on a rock and he reached out to steady me, but I righted myself before he could take my arm. Thanking him in French, I prepared to move on.

Walid, however, didn't move. A light in the passage behind him made a rough halo of his curls, but his face remained steeped in shadow.

"It's so easy for us to speak when we're walking," he remarked, "but at home you rarely look my way."

I became aware of his height, the lateness of the hour, and that we were alone in the high-walled passage. I took a step back, feeling rough brick just behind me.

Instantly he understood. "Please don't be afraid," he said, switching to Berber. "I didn't mean to —" he broke off and turned his face to the light.

Seeing that he was troubled, I waited, still wary. He stared into a storefront, then glanced back down at me. "I only wanted to tell you that —" again he stopped speaking.

Walid was wearing a denim jacket, and he hunched his shoulders against the breeze. "It's cold as a pharaoh's tomb out here! This is stupid. I'm sorry. Let's go home."

We passed the store where Hania and I purchased our clothes. The mannequins watched us with stony eyes. Two men in dark robes approached, complaining loudly about a football match. Walid moved closer as they passed.

"I don't mean to frighten you," he said softly, returning to French. "I enjoy your company. I tell you things I don't share with others. Still, I feel I hardly know you."

Unsure how to answer, I remained silent. His deep voice was hushed, swallowed by the enclosing walls.

"You're a mystery, Leila. You learned to read and write the way the sand soaks in the tide. You've changed the fortunes of our business, and you've even brought out the patience and kindness in my wildcat of a sister.

"But what I find most extraordinary," he said, his words barely more than a whisper, "is how you manage to make peace with your past."

Sweat beaded my forehead, and I grew dizzier with each step. I tried to walk faster, but fear of falling slowed my progress. Walid continued to speak, unaware of my distress.

"Leila, I saw that village where you were born. I heard the fear in the voice of the woman living in your parents' house, and saw the jealousy and cruelty of that old man in the store. I can't begin to imagine how it must have felt to learn that your family simply vanished, without leaving any way for you to find them."

Now I stopped walking. I stared at Walid's silhouette a few steps ahead. His words opened wounds I struggled to seal deeper away than even my most painful memories of Essaouira.

"I know," he continued, "you've experienced things you've never told anyone. I know your sleep is troubled because those things still live so close to the surface of your mind. I also know that, despite the years you've lived with us, you are deathly afraid of me — even at this moment."

"I'm sorry," I gasped, my voice stretched close to breaking.

"Sorry?" he echoed. "For what?" He paused, and turning to look at me, his voice softened. "You show my mother so much love, no one would ever guess how little love has been shown to you. And you continue to rise, morning after morning after morning, knowing the people who hurt you might still be searching for you —"

I cried out softly and he moved into the light, where I could clearly see his face.

"I only wish," he said, "I knew how to help you."

A long moment passed as a kind of door creaked open in my mind. Slowly, I lifted my hand and placed it on the center of his chest. Walid pressed his hands tight over mine. Though I felt hope throbbing there beneath my fingers, I wasn't sure if I was reaching for his heart, or pushing it away.

4. Scars

2012

After that night, something eased between us. I began to enjoy our Wednesday walks through the souk, and was only mildly nervous when Walid asked whether I'd mind stopping at *Sidi Saidi*, the shop where he purchased his books. He said the owner, a friend from his days as a student, had called to say a book he ordered had arrived from France, and he could pick it up.

We strolled through a quarter of the city I'd never visited, a few streets from the university. Beardless men in blue jeans, and women in short skirts sat together in cafes, smoking cigarettes, sipping coffee and talking enthusiastically.

Few of the women wore headscarves, and many had their hair cut short, hennaed to autumn red or streaked with blonde. They wore sharp, lemony perfumes and much of their conversation was in French.

When we entered the shop I paused at the threshold, peering around in awe. Listing shelves from the floor to the ceiling stood packed with books of all kinds, written in French, Arabic and a language that was, perhaps, English. Some volumes were thicker than building bricks; others would fit into the palm of my hand. The air was warm with the scents of aging leather and fresh coffee, and Rajae Belmlih's rich voice poured from hidden speakers.

A second room, then a third followed. Stacked end-to-end, I wondered how anyone could find anything in such a place. Then I realized searching was part of the pleasure: one would go on a hunt for a certain jewel, only to find an even more valuable, unexpected treasure along the way.

Walid's face brightened and his eyes, so often filled with shadow, seemed to clear. A slender man in jeans with a head full of wild curls, but no moustache or beard, came from behind the counter to greet him. His piercing, light brown eyes seemed vaguely familiar, like a fragment of my past in Essaouira. I instinctively slipped behind Walid, hoping the man wouldn't notice me. To my dismay, Walid turned and tipped his head politely in my direction.

"Leila, this is my friend, Amin."

Amin responded warmly, as if he knew of me already. "I hope you enjoyed the book of poetry. Walid tells me you come from the region just south of Marrakech."

"—Yes," I stammered.

"I suppose you left home to come to the big city," he replied, laughing lightly. "I myself was born in Essaouira, but my parents took us to live in France when we were quite small."

"Can you imagine it?" Walid said, shaking his head. "His parents manage to send their children to French universities, and as soon as they graduate, Amin and his sisters move right back to the place where their parents started."

My startled silence caused both men to look at me in concern. Walid spoke first. "What is it, Leila?"

Choosing my words carefully, I addressed the bookstore owner.

"I lived in Essaouira before coming here, and I knew two sisters who ran a women's center there."

"You've met Fatima and Aisha?" Amin asked, his smile deepening into a grin. "They live here in Casablanca, now."

Amin looked back at Walid. "My sisters are rebels, my friend. They tried to modernize Essaouira and got escorted out of town by the authorities. They're planning to open a center here as soon as they find a suitable space." Amin reached for a paper, adding, "I'll write down their phone numbers so you can call them. They'll be very pleased to hear from you, I'm sure."

My heart soared as I took the paper. My mother often said that a friend is another self. Aisha and Fatima were the first friends I'd ever known.

As we walked home that night, Walid suggested I write my story. Inside I laughed at the idea, thinking that no one would care what had befallen a girl from an unknown corner of the Atlas Mountains. I imagined, as always, that Walid was just being kind.

And yet that night, as I lay awake, thinking of the call I would make the next day, I wondered if perhaps he was right. I fell asleep imagining how it would feel to write a book, and dreamed I was warmed by the sun making flutes of the tall grasses swaying beside a swiftly flowing river.

"Today we must have your *very* best," Selina insisted as Walid helped Younes, the delivery man, unload the usual crates of milk, sugar, eggs, and flour from his truck.

Younes laughed and handed Walid another crate. "We always bring you nothing but our best, Selina!"

"Did you remember the rosewater?"

"This must, indeed, be a special day," he said, reaching inside the cabin for a brightly labeled bottle.

"Tonight," Selina declared, "we're celebrating new members of our family!"

Indeed, that afternoon we closed the tearoom early; Selina's favorite butcher from the souk had delivered an enormous slab of freshly slaughtered mutton, and while Shada and Aliah baked, I prepared the dishes I loved most from my days in the kitchen of the house of pleasure: quince and honey *tajïne* stewed with butter and cinnamon, rice pudding with a hint of rosewater, and a rich apple-sauce cake.

While cooking, I listened to Shada and Aliah gossip about the stars of their favorite television programs. As the afternoon progressed, I also watched the people walking up the causeway.

Two evenings before, with Selina at my side, I nervously pressed the numbers on the telephone. We brought our heads close to listen as the phone rang once, twice, three times.

A woman answered.

"Are you — I mean, am I speaking to Aisha?" I asked shyly.

"Yes, this is Aisha. Who's calling?"

"I am Leila. Leila from Essaouira."

Like a shutter blown open by a great gust, I heard her shout: "Leila? God is great! Where are you? When can we see you?"

Now a battered truck, a broom and mop painted on its side, growled along the boulevard, spewing blue-black clouds of exhaust. As the fumes cleared, two figures emerged, striding briskly toward the tearoom.

Neither woman wore a *djellaba* or headscarf; Aisha's lavender scarf draped loosely over her shoulders and her violet skirt was short enough to reveal her boots, whose buckles flashed in the sunlight. Her hair, once short, now bounced in shining dark curls past her shoulders.

Fatima, the taller and leaner of the two, wore wide-legged black trousers. Her ivory sweater was clasped at the waist by a thick belt, and her chestnut hair was rolled into a loose braid, with strands blowing free in the sea breeze. She was the first to cross our threshold; I had already come into the tearoom and stood waiting with tears in my eyes.

I did not weep alone: Fatima ran the last steps toward me, took my face in her hands, kissed my cheeks, and swept me into a hug that grew tighter when Aisha joined in.

"You've gained weight," Fatima declared.

"But not nearly enough," Aisha added.

Suddenly the three of us were laughing. I turned toward Selina, who smiled warmly from the counter. Hania stood beside her mother, eyes flickering protectively between the sisters and me.

"Five years," Fatima whispered, her eyes fixed on my face. "We have prayed for you every day for the past five years."

"And I have thanked you in my heart every moment since we last met," I replied.

We ate slowly, with several tables pushed together to accommodate our family and guests, including Shada, Aliah, Rachid, and Hania's two sons.

In time, Hania gathered up her boys and Rachid loaded them into their car. Shada and Aliah left so as not to miss their bus.

Despite my protests, the sisters rose to help us clear the dishes. Walid remained in the tearoom to wipe down the tables, and I found myself in the kitchen, encircled by the three women — Fatima, Aisha and Selina — who'd saved my life.

"Please tell us what happened the last time we met," Aisha began softly, eyes fixed on my scar, "— the day you tried to escape from Essaouira."

"Our cousin said a policeman recognized you at the city gates," Fatima added. "Was there nothing he could have done to stop them from taking you?"

"I'm sorry to have caused you to worry," I answered, "but no one could have helped. The police held me until a servant arrived from my Master's house. My Young Master's wedding had taken place that evening. There were many guests, and much work to be done. They were very angry that I hadn't come home, so —" I touched my scar.

"It was our fault!" Fatima exclaimed. "We should never have encouraged you to leave!"

"No, *habiba*," I replied, hearing the anguish in her voice. "You and Aisha were the only people who told me that no one had the right to hold me against my will. You said it was against the law, against our faith, and that I hadn't given my consent. I'd never even heard the word *consent* before."

"But Leila, your face —"

"— Is a small price to pay for my freedom."

"Still, we should have tried to assist you by legal means. It was reckless to send you away with someone you didn't know."

"Fatima's right," Aisha agreed. "Our cousin has never forgiven himself for what happened that evening."

"Yet," I replied, "those few moments of freedom gave me the courage to try again."

I told them about Young Master's threat, and how I'd decided suddenly, with no real plan, to disguise myself in Young Mistress' clothing and simply vanish into the city. I described how the simple kindness of strangers brought me to Casablanca, and to the safety of Selina's door.

"You had no difficulty at the police checkpoint?" Fatima asked in wonder.

"No."

She smiled sardonically. "The guard was afraid to question you, because you were with Europeans."

"And because you were dressed in the clothes of a wealthy woman," Aisha guessed, raising an eyebrow. "If you'd been wearing a *djellaba* —"

"I might be dead today."

"We, too, had to flee Essaouira," Aisha said. "The authorities claimed we were encouraging women to disrespect their husbands and fathers. They accused us of other things, as well, which are too ridiculous to repeat."

"We were given thirty minutes to pack our belongings or face arrest," Fatima added. "They wanted to keep our computer, but we managed to get it into our cousin's car before they realized we'd taken it. They followed us to the city gates and promised to arrest us if we return. Imagine: we've been banished from the city of our birth!"

I thought about other women I'd seen in the Center, hiding their faces from view, clearly ashamed or afraid to be identified. How many were still trapped, with no idea how to be freed?

"What will you do now?" Selina asked.

"We thought about opening a center here," Fatima answered, "but a friend has asked me to write for a new magazine about women in our country, called *The Voice*. We're hoping to reach readers throughout North Africa and France."

"And I've been offered a teaching position at the university," Aisha said. "It's just a few courses, but I'll have time to continue my community work. Which reminds me —"

She reached into her bag and lifted out a slim package wrapped in silver paper. "Our brother told us you enjoy poetry. This book was written by a poet in America, and translated into French. I hope you'll like it."

I accepted the gift shyly. When I removed the paper, a woman with fierce eyes stared back.

"This poet has been a great inspiration to us," Fatima explained. "She writes that we must speak, even when we're afraid, because the powerful do not intend for us to survive."

After a film one night, Walid guided me to our usual table at the café near the cinema. As we sat, two young men at a neighboring table stared openly. I was used to this; my scarred face presented mirrored halves of the handsome and hideous. Often, when I shopped in the souk or served customers in the tearoom, I marked their reactions when, after seeing my right side in profile, I simply turned my head. Some gasped. Others looked away in discomfort. Occasionally, children pointed and their mothers hushed them.

Now I turned my body so my left side was in shadow. Walid, however, addressed the men directly.

"Good evening," I heard him say. "Have we met before?"

They muttered a reply, but he persisted.

"You were looking at us as if you wished to speak. Is there something I can do for you?"

The tension in his voice was unmistakable, and they mumbled apologies, rose and walked away.

Walid's body relaxed. He picked up a menu and glanced at it. "Shall we have ice-cream this evening, instead of our usual glass of tea?"

"No, thank you," I answered. Only his eyes registered his lingering anger.

"Walid, please don't trouble yourself —"

"Their rudeness was inexcusable."

"I don't blame them. No one knows how to react to something like this." I touched my cheek.

"You speak as if you were some kind of monster."

"My mother often said that god lets some people learn through joy and laughter, while others must learn through pain and sorrow. I must accept the path life has given me."

He set the menu down, and his expression darkened.

"Leila," he said in a tone so low that no one at the neighboring tables would hear him, but so clear I could make out every word, "don't you understand why that man did this to your face?"

"He did it to punish me for trying to escape."

"No," Walid replied, leaning close. "That was only his excuse. It's true that he marked you for capture, should you ever again attempt to leave. But his real purpose was to carve your slavery into your flesh. He wanted to be sure you'd never feel you deserve to be treated like a full human being.

"Dear sister," he continued, "that man wanted you to see something broken and ugly in the mirror, so you'd hate yourself. He isolated you from others, so you'd believe your only purpose was to obey him without thought or question.

"But the worst is this: he maimed your face so you'd never seek to love, or be loved. You'd never dare to dream about becoming a wife and mother, or to know the safety of a family. He wanted you to live in the shadows, always hiding, and always afraid. He wanted you to believe that the rest of the world sees you through his eyes.

"But understand this: He failed. Despite everything they did to you in Essaouira, you're sitting here, on this terrace, tonight.

"Leila, your face is everything you've suffered and survived. You must never be ashamed. You're more beautiful than I can possibly describe."

I lay awake that night, faced with an unfamiliar emotion. I had no words for it, and I didn't dare to believe it. It made me more afraid than I had ever been before.

Suddenly my heart sped up each time Walid entered the room. I wanted to be near him all the time. My breath caught in my throat when he looked into my eyes. I found myself smiling for no reason, and knew neither hunger, nor fatigue.

And Walid himself, who only weeks before had rarely spoken, now never ceased to speak.

He'd drive Selina and me to the tearoom before dawn, describing in humorous detail his deliveries to the hospitals and schools that purchased our bread. He'd walk past the stove where I was grilling almonds, joking about things the tourists said. After our evening prayers, he'd sit across from Selina and me in the apartment, reminiscing about his childhood adventures in the *souk*. Most of the boys from his past had followed their fathers and brothers to look for work in France, never to return.

"I wonder what keeps them there," he mused aloud. "Everything is expensive, jobs are scarce, and it rains all the time."

"But everyone says Paris is beautiful," I offered.

"Yes," he agreed, "there are parks and fountains and the Eiffel Tower is, indeed, impressive. It is also true that some French people live very well. Many of our people, however, are forced to live outside the city in areas filled with violence and crime.

"Still, I wonder what you would make of Paris. Perhaps we'll all visit one day."

Many evenings I accompanied Walid to Amin's bookstore, where I enjoyed tea with Aisha and Fatima. As we walked through the *souk* he described the books he wanted to read. He was fascinated by the history of the Berber people, and spoke of his fear that our culture was vanishing as we left the mountains for city life.

As our conversations continued, I also began to speak more freely, and even to laugh out loud — though I was always surprised by the sound of my own laughter.

Walid laughed, too.

"You must be very careful of this one," he warned me as he passed through the kitchen one morning, gesturing toward his sister. "I'm sure she's looking for new ways to out-bake you."

"Don't be ridiculous!" Hania snapped. "I'd never even try."

"That's only because you're too busy gossiping about where French supermodels buy their shoes."

"There is nothing wrong with having a sense of fashion!"

"Shoes belong on your feet, not in your dreams."

"You dress like a grandfather, Walid! You should let me take you shopping."

"What you put in the kettle ends up on your spoon. I prefer to spend money on —"

"I know: books!"

And he began to sing. Not Berber songs, like Selina, and he never sang anything all the way through. Instead, we'd hear Walid whistling a melody from the radio as he brought supplies into the workroom, humming softly as he prepared sandwiches for customers, or chanting his favorite songs in the shower.

"This may be hard for you to believe," Hania explained one morning after he left to make the deliveries, "but Walid was a happy boy. After supper he'd act out things he'd seen in the *souk* and keep us laughing all evening. He'd make up silly words to the songs on the radio, and sing them while he studied. He loved going to movies and telling us the stories as if they'd happened in Casablanca. He had a great imagination and a big, wonderful smile."

Hania spread almond paste on a layer of thin, sugared dough. "It's as if my brother was lost and now, after ages, he's finding his way back to himself."

If Selina noticed any change in her son, her small face offered no sign. She still teased him lovingly, ignored his silent days, and vanished each time she noticed he was speaking to me alone.

One evening after we closed I stood behind the tearoom, watching the sun slip into the sea. I became aware of Walid's presence beside me.

"So this is why you feel so little need to speak," he observed, echoing something said to me once, long before. "Your soul is at peace when you're near the sea."

5.   Desert Rain

The woman's brown curls swept her shoulders, and a cream-colored sweater fell loosely to her waist. Her son, who must have been about four, sat close beside her, coloring pictures with a bright red crayon. His sticky glass was half-full, and his sweet roll lay abandoned. She watched him lovingly as she sipped her tea.

As I bent to pick up a tray I caught sight of Walid, who stood behind the counter, his gaze fixed on the woman and her child. His face, normally professional and polite, was clouded by such intense anguish that I was instantly afraid.

Selina, working by the cash register, followed my gaze. She set down the cloth she used to wipe the tables, and walked over to Walid. Speaking quietly, she nudged him gently toward the rear of the tearoom. Then she turned to me. No words between us were needed.

I found him standing behind the building, facing the water. It was a hot, windy day and gusts of the *sirocco* sent his hair into an awkward dance. He had removed his apron and crossed his arms tightly over his chest. A cigarette burned, forgotten, between his clenched fingers.

I came up and stood beside him in silence. Children's voices echoed from the beach, and truck horns blared on the causeway behind us. When he didn't speak, I turned to go.

"No, wait —" he said quickly. "I'm sorry. It's difficult when we draw near the dates when they died."

The wind whipped my scarf loose and I reached up to clear the hair from my face.

"Leila, I want you to know the truth about Nora and me."

Our eyes met, and for the first time it was Walid who looked away.

"You've heard, I'm sure, about my beautiful wife. My mother and sister have certainly told you how deeply happy we were. But there is no land without stones."

He stared out over the water.

"We met in the university courtyard. Nora was reading a book, and I sat down beside her to study. We began talking and I thought we'd never stop. She loved learning new things and was excited about becoming a teacher."

Walid looked at the memory, smiling briefly.

"Nora told me the day we met that her father opposed her studies. He had already selected her husband, and wanted her to marry and start a family. He thought it was dangerous for her to attend the university, surrounded by men. He feared Nora would no longer remain true to her faith, or respect the traditions of our people, and threatened to disown her if she disobeyed."

My eyes widened, and Walid nodded. "Yes, Leila, even here there are men who refuse their daughters the right to study. Nora gave up her family to remain at the university — and to be with me."

He again turned to the water. Driven by the wind, cresting waves crashed again and again into the seawall.

"When we married, we knew we were bringing dishonor on her family. My parents were deeply concerned, but they could not dissuade us. Nora pretended not to care, but I knew it hurt her very much that she was lost to her mother and sisters. She never spoke of it, but she was no longer whole.

"Imagine, Leila: she had no one at our wedding. Her letters to them went unanswered. Though my mother and Hania tried to fill that void, no one could replace them."

Walid picked up a shell that lay near his feet and examined it blindly.

"Nora wanted to start a family right away, though I thought it was too soon to have a child. I was working in the bakery and trying to finish my studies, and there was hardly enough room for the two of us, even without a baby, in my parents' apartment. But Nora thought her father might forgive her once she bore a grandchild, and then her mother and sisters would be part of her life once more."

He rolled his head from side to side to release his tension.

"Nora became ill during the second half of her pregnancy, but she refused to stay in bed. She was trying to finish her studies as fast as possible so she could begin to teach. She thought that once she was working, we could afford an apartment of our own.

"She went into labor two months early. I rushed her to the hospital, but the baby was breech — turned backwards in her womb — and they couldn't stop the bleeding. Nora died within minutes of the birth, and our son died two days later.

"During her labor, Nora asked me to telephone her home so she could apologize to her father. I called, but when he realized who I was, he hung up. No one from her family ever acknowledged her death. They behaved as if she'd never been born."

Walid threw the shell and watched as it arced toward the seawall, landing soundlessly in the water.

"After their deaths I couldn't eat, sleep, or even speak. My father took over the morning deliveries, because I couldn't get out of bed. He became ill after a very cold night and died of pneumonia a few days later.

"I lost my father because I caused Nora to lose hers. I knew it was wrong to marry over her father's objections. I knew it was wrong for her to abandon her family to be with me. But all I could think about was how much I loved her, and how badly I wanted her to be my wife.

"Dishonor breeds dishonor, Leila. My wife, son and father paid for my weakness with their lives."

The wind picked up, sending a paper cup bouncing toward us. A gull swept by, calling shrilly to its mate. The voices of the children playing in the sand grew sharper. For a long time neither of us spoke.

Hesitantly I touched his arm.

"I can't speak about the past, Walid, but I believe you honor them by taking care of Selina and Hania. You honored them when you took me to my village to help me search for my mother."

"Yes, but I failed with that, too."

"No, Walid. When I saw the village, I understood what my life would have been had I remained. Though we didn't find my mother, I'm glad she's not living there in sickness or hunger."

I looked out over the water.

"Truthfully, I feel my mother is still with me. If you listen closely, you'll find that Nora's still with you, too. She wouldn't want you to remember her in bitterness and shame. I think she'd want you to seek some contentment in your life."

"Perhaps," he said, "she led me to you."

"To me?" Suddenly the sea, the birds, the children — were soundless. All I could hear was his voice.

"I lived in darkness until the day I came home and found you in my mother's kitchen. I sensed your intelligence, which you protect with humility. I felt your fear, which made me wonder who'd hurt you. I could see how much you mean to my mother, because, I think, you remind her of herself when she was a girl."

He moved closer. "Leila, I don't know what we'd do if you left us."

"I don't want to leave."

"No. I don't know what I'd do if you left *me*. If you stay, I swear that I will never, ever cause you pain."

"Walid, I —"

"Leila, I'm asking you to marry me."

"Marry you?"

"Please be my wife," he said. "Neither the sun in winter, nor rain in the desert would make me happier."

"I can't marry anyone."

"You don't have to be afraid. I would never hurt you."

"No, it's not possible," I said, backing away.

"But why?"

"Because I'm not like other women!"

"Leila —"

"Please don't, Walid. I will never be any man's wife."

When I entered the tearoom Selina looked up expectantly. I tried to smile and failed. Picking up the tray, I backed into the kitchen and continued my work. I didn't see Walid until that night, after we closed. He brought in our usual shipment of flour and sugar, and quietly wished us all goodnight.

Then the clouds came, and autumn storms sent waves battering the seawall, and rain slashing at the windows. The tearoom filled with students and older people who sat for hours reading books, playing backgammon, or debating the newspaper headlines. I continued to stock the display cases, and Selina moved between the tables, charming our guests. Walid sold fewer sandwiches, so he kept himself busy reorganizing the storage area.

Selina watched the sudden distance between us and said nothing. Hania asked me repeatedly why her brother and I had again become strangers. I answered them both with a shrug and went back to my work.

On Wednesday evenings I found Walid waiting for me after class, as usual. He kept pace with my troubled stride, and protectively scrutinized the people we passed. He asked about the class, as was his habit, and complimented my continuing progress.

One evening we came out of the narrow passage and I could see the old bakery, lights on in the windows of the apartment upstairs, where Selina waited.

"Leila," Walid said as we approached the door, "there's one other thing I didn't have the chance to tell you that day on the beach."

"Yes?"

He grasped the door handle, which had a brass knocker in the shape of a lion's head. "I love you."

The greatest threat to love is the fear of losing that love. Nothing in my life had prepared me for the possibility of loving a man. My father sold me to my abductors in payment for his debts. My Master in Essaouira believed I had no needs or desires. For years his servant beat me, and his son raped me. When I finally escaped from Essaouira, I feared men more than anything on earth.

During the day I watched Walid as never before. I saw local women linger near the counter, tossing a few words to him as he served others. Kohl-lined eyes followed him as he went about his work, seeking to capture his gaze.

Frenchwomen were drawn to him, too. Tourists entered the tearoom from the beach, smelling of peppery lemon and coconut oil, thin wraps barely hiding their breasts, and only the smallest of coverings below. Some appeared several times a day and asked Walid the time, or for directions to a certain store, or just for a glass of cool water.

I looked on, bemused, as they showed off their fine necks, perfect feet and lean, sun-browned thighs. I knew Walid could have any one of them for an afternoon, a night, or forever.

Yet each morning before daybreak he met me with exactly the same calm greeting as the day before. Every Wednesday he was waiting when my class was over. He continued to invite me to see films and accompany him to the bookstore. No more was said of marriage, or love.

There was nothing more to be said.

I went on each day, watching and waiting and hoping for some sign of what to do. When I passed a mirror I searched for myself in the reflection, but a woman with hollow eyes stared back. I listened to the sea more closely as I went about my work, but the waves told me nothing.

Hania's voice became the sound of insistent bees. Selina's face seemed as remote as the women on the television. Even Fatima and Aisha were of little interest to me. I lived among them, yet I was miles and miles away.

Madame Chafik asked me to stay behind a few weeks later, when the others filed out at the end of class. I approached her desk as she placed her belongings in her bag.

"Is anything wrong, Leila?"

"No, Madame," I replied in French, "but thank you for asking."

She paused, book in hand. "I've been teaching you for more than a year, and I've watched you grow more confident with every class. Several weeks ago something changed, and even though your body's still here, your thoughts seem far away."

"I will try to do better."

"Oh, Leila. Both your comprehension and speaking abilities are fine."

I peered at my teacher, whose eyes saw me in ways I couldn't see myself. I looked away.

"I apologize," I said, with a backward step toward the door.

"Leila, stay for a moment and talk to me."

"I can't —"

"Why not?"

"He's waiting."

"Who's waiting?"

"Walid. If I make him wait, he might leave."

"I see," she said. "Is Walid your husband?"

"Of course not — I mean, he's — he's like a brother to me."

"Is he always in a rush to get home?"

"No," I replied honestly.

"But you think he'd be angry if you spent a few extra minutes with me?"

"I don't know, now that —" I broke off.

"Now that what, Leila?"

"Now that I refused to marry him," I said, rushing the words.

Madame Chafik set her book down gently. "Was the marriage arranged by your families?"

"No."

"Would your families oppose it?"

"Not at all."

"Do you care for him?"

I started to nod, then vigorously shook my head.

"How long have you known him?"

"Almost six years."

"Is he kind to you?

"Yes."

"Do you think he cares for you?"

"He was married before, but she died. I know he still loves her very much."

"Has he said this to you?"

"No, but I see it in his eyes."

Madame Chafik smiled. "The heart of a fool is in his mouth; the mouth of a wise man is in his heart. Leila, perhaps it's difficult for him to express what he feels."

"He told me he loves me."

"Then why did you refuse?"

When I didn't answer she reached across the desk and held out her hand. I took it, surprised at the current that passed between us.

"The scars people see," she said gently, "are often mere shadows of the wounds we feel inside. Some say what we learn in childhood is engraved in the stone of our hearts. I believe, however, that though it is very difficult, the hardest stone can be shaped into an exquisite sculpture.

"Leila, perhaps the only way to heal is to take this chance, even if it frightens you."

"He deserves better," I whispered, admitting my greatest fear.

"Better?" she repeated in surprise.

"Madame Chafik, I have nothing at all to give him."

"Perhaps, sweet child, giving yourself is enough."

We stood in silence long enough to hear the custodian lock the room next door. Gently she released my hand and lifted her book bag.

"We'd better go now. I don't want to spend the night here, and I also suspect that someone who cares very deeply about you is waiting outside."

Walid was, indeed, standing near the door. He stepped into the light as I said goodnight to my teacher, who nodded with the trace of a smile and disappeared.

That night I slept without ghosts from my past, and when I rose and knelt before dawn the next morning, my mind was clear.

I put away my prayer rug and descended the stairs. Walid was waiting, with Selina, at the rear door. There was something different in my gait, or the set of my shoulders, or perhaps in my face. Walid opened his mouth to greet me and his eyes met mine.

And he smiled. Even without words, he understood. He opened his arms and welcomed me inside.

6.   ROCKROSES

"You don't officially exist," Walid announced one evening several weeks before our wedding.

"When I went to apply for our marriage license, I realized you have no identity papers. I explained to the clerk that you were born in a village, and no birth certificate was ever issued. He said we must apply for one, now, and that we can seek a marriage license once your birth certificate has been approved."

Selina looked over Walid's shoulder. "I didn't need such papers when I married your father."

"Those were simpler times, Mother. Today the government keeps records of everything."

"When I fill out these papers," I said, "the police will know how to find me."

Walid took my hand. "Leila, tell me as much as you can about the people who are looking for you."

"My Master is a judge named Senhaji Yusef Hakim, and his son is called Senhaji Nassim Rachid."

"What do they know about you?"

For a moment I was confused by his question. Then I realized that, indeed, my captors in Essaouira had no more asked me about my family, birthplace, or birthday, than one might ask those things of a dog.

"The judge called me Rana, but his son first knew me as Hajar. Eventually, though, he asked and I told him my father called me Leila."

"But does he know your surname — the name of your father?"

"No. I doubt that anyone knew my father's surname — even the men who took me away."

"And the name of your village?"

"The men told my first Mistress nothing, except that no one would come looking for me. She immediately changed my name, saying Leila was the name of a daughter, and I was a daughter no more."

Selina walked to the window so I couldn't see her face.

"Then you must name yourself," Walid said quietly.

"And select a birthdate of your choosing," Selina added.

"But if I don't use my father's name, my family will never find me."

There was an uncomfortable silence, followed by the sound of Walid clearing his throat. "Leila, I don't think your father is looking for you."

"No, but god willing, one day my mother or brothers might try."

"She's right," Selina said. "No mother would ever stop wondering what became of her daughter."

"If we use your father's name," Walid responded, "someone might trace you to your village, even if it seems unlikely."

Selina returned to the table. "Why not use your mother's family name? That way you'd still have some ties to her people."

"My mother's brothers forced her to marry my father, then did nothing to help when my father could no longer feed us. I can't honor them in this way. And I think it would be a mistake to give anyone the name of my village."

"Yes," Walid agreed, "it might be better to use the largest city possible. Though the government has few records of the inhabitants of the Berber villages, the people themselves have long memories."

I thought of the shopkeeper in my village, who once asked my father to marry me to his son. It was he who told us of my family's departure from the village, when we went back to find them.

Walid spread the forms on the table and handed me a pen. "You're free to create your own identity, Leila."

"I don't know what name to choose."

"Think of a name," he replied, "that frees you from your past, but honors your survival."

Hania would not hear of me wearing a Berber wedding dress, with layers of gauzy fabric draped over my shoulders and around my waist. "She'll look like a little girl playing dress-up with the curtains."

Selina, however, said I would be beautiful in the deep red headscarf, dangling silver jewelry and gold-threaded cloaks traditionally worn by mountain brides.

"The wedding crown will bring out her lovely green eyes!"

"Leila doesn't live in the mountains, Mother."

"We should be proud of our Berber traditions!"

"I'm proud to be Berber," Hania argued, "but no bride wants to look like she's being traded for a cow!"

If the mother and sister hoped Walid would settle their argument, their hopes were in vain. He smiled calmly and suggested I wear whatever I liked.

"But Walid —" Hania began.

"Your brother is right," Selina said. "And more importantly, the decision is Leila's to make."

Both women then looked at me. I glanced at all three.

"Hania," I said, "before I decide I'll let you take me shopping."

This, however, led to the next argument.

"I'm going to rent a hall and hire the best musicians in Casablanca to entertain our guests!" Selina declared. "I've started a list of which vendors in the *souk* we can count on for the freshest fruit and vegetables, and I've already spoken with Tahar the butcher about purchasing two sheep for the celebration."

When I spoke of the cost, she took my face in her hands and chortled joyfully.

"Kindness plucks the hairs of the lion's mane. We have many people to thank for our tearoom's success. This is the wedding of my only son and my youngest daughter — well, perhaps I should say this wedding will *make* you my youngest daughter — and no expense will be spared!"

"Selina, I'm honored and very grateful for everything you've planned, but I'm also afraid that a large wedding will bring me too much attention."

"That's nonsense!" Hania exclaimed. "No one would find anything strange about Walid marrying someone who's lived and worked with our family for years."

"Perhaps," Walid replied, "but some will ask where Leila came from, and why none of her family is present."

"We'll say she came from Rabat and her parents are no longer living."

"And they'll wonder about my appearance," I added.

"There's nothing wrong with your face," Hania insisted.

"I thank you, Sister, but my scar invites the eye like sugar calls the tongue. I'm a stranger whose face tells her story."

"And those who know little repeat it often," Walid agreed. "A room's door can be shut, unlike the mouth of a fool."

"Are you suggesting we cancel?" Hania asked. "Mother's already planned everything!"

"The plans," Walid replied, "are Leila's to approve. She mustn't feel uncomfortable at her own wedding."

Selina looked from her son to me. "Leila, do you truly feel fearful about being seen by so many people?"

"Yes. I'm sorry, Mother. I only want to be with my friends and my family."

"I agree," Walid concurred.

Hania raised her hands in exasperation. "I wish Rachid agreed so often with me! Look at them — they're two stones in a wall!"

"Yes," Selina laughed as she tore her wedding plans in half, "and that's only the *first* reason they belong together."

A few evenings later Selina came to my bedroom door and led me by the hand into her own room. A photograph of a slender, dark-haired man with deep brown eyes hung over the dresser.

"I still miss him, after all this time," she remarked as she walked to her wardrobe. With a wave of her arm she gestured for me to sit on the bed, which was covered with a flowered spread. Other photographs of young Hania and Walid covered a chest of drawers. I could see from the photos how much Hania resembled her father.

Selina returned with a zippered bag and a box that she laid beside me. Carefully she unzipped the bag to reveal a dress of very fine, crème-colored silk. The neck was cut high to rise up along the throat, and the wide, gathered sleeves were cuffed at the wrist. Hand-stitched, delicate pink rockroses began at the shoulders and became interwoven over the heart. The bodice was cut for a slender woman with a long, thin waist.

Lifting the dress out of the bag, Selina let the pleated skirt unfold, like lotus petals in a river breeze. A fine vest of dusty rose silk matched the embroidery.

"I wore this at my wedding thirty-five years ago, when I was fifteen," Selina said. "There was never any question of Hania wearing it — she was too large! But now you can see I was as slender as you when I was a bride."

Carefully I touched a sleeve. Selina smiled wistfully.

"My parents brought me down from our mountain village, by mule, to buy it. We got to Marrakech and had no idea how to find the tailor. The streets were so noisy and packed with people! Fortunately, one of our cousins met us at the mosque and brought us to her house.

"The tailor was a very old Berber woman who sat in her window all day, sewing in the sun. She told me I had pretty eyes. Then she took a long red cord and measured me. I was terribly nervous!"

Selina laughed. "We came back several weeks later to pick up the dress. I had never seen anything so beautiful! I have no idea to this day how my father managed to pay her. I didn't try it on until the morning of the wedding. Fortunately, it fit me perfectly. Only then did I truly understand how gifted a seamstress she was."

Selina sank down beside me on the bed. "Leila, you cannot imagine what it was like to marry a man you had seen only once, with both sets of parents looking on. I knew how to cook and wash and sew, but no one had told me the secrets of married life.

"Even worse, he wanted to take me away from our village to Casablanca, a place I'd barely heard of. The night before the wedding I crawled into bed with three of my sisters, and when my aunts came to help me dress, they shrieked! My eyes were so swollen I looked like I'd been possessed by a *djinn*!"

Selina opened the box and peeled back layers of tissue paper. She took out a pair of pearl-colored shoes with glass jewels at the toes. "Aren't they lovely? My mother's sister made a gift of them to me. I loved them so much I wore them all day inside the house. I even tried to sleep in them one night.

"Please try on the dress, and the shoes, too, if you'd like. No one has touched them for years. I would love to see them worn, even if only tonight."

Selina left, closing the door firmly behind her. Alone, I stepped out of my light robe and stood for a moment, peering at the dress. It was, indeed, the most beautiful dress I'd ever seen, and more importantly, Selina had worn it on her wedding day.

I lifted and dropped it gingerly over my shoulders. Falling easily to my waist, the skirt drifted soundlessly to the floor. I slipped my arms into the sleeves and pulled the neckline over my shoulders. Small though it was, the dress was still too loose in the waist and several inches too long, but the shoulders and bust fit perfectly.

I heard a soft knock and the door opened behind me. Selina let out a cry and clasped her hands.

"Don't move — let me button you up," she said, dancing across the room. "Now, close your eyes until I tell you to look!" I felt the dress shift against my body, then I was turned to face the mirror.

Selina gathered up my hair and pinned it back from my face. She took something from a drawer and tied it carefully around my head.

"Open your eyes," she said.

I didn't recognize the woman who looked back at me. Perhaps for the first time in my life I saw myself as Walid must have seen me — not as a damaged, ever-fearful creature, but rather as a woman with some beauty, strength and purpose.

Selina stepped back.

"Leila, I haven't been deaf to my daughter's words about your wedding dress. This is an important day in your life, and I'll understand if this dress doesn't make your heart sing. For me, it is pleasure enough to see it worn, at least once more, by someone I love."

I smiled at her in the mirror. "Might it be worn a second time, Mother? I'd be honored to wear it on the day I truly become your daughter."

On the eve of the ceremony Selina remained in my room late into the night. I'd spent the evening resting while Selina, Hania, Fatima and Aisha decorated our hands and feet with intricate henna designs, and told me many stories of other weddings, both tragic and glorious. They then turned their attention to my hair, which they hennaed a softer auburn, then washed in rosewater. I was fed stuffed dates and *haloua dial jeljlane*, sesame seeds in honey, my favorite patisserie, and we drank iced apple, banana and melon juices.

After the others departed, Selina laid down beside me in the gathering dark and spoke softly, her fingers laced gently through mine.

"I remember how lost I was when my husband and I first arrived in Casablanca. We had no family or friends here, and we'd only been married a few days. He told my father he was bringing me to my own house, where I'd have everything I could ask for. But when we arrived, he had to hire a man with a mule to carry our bags from the train station, all the way through the *souk*, to our new home.

"We walked for what seemed like hours along the muddy passageways, with everyone around us speaking Arabic, and I asked him in Berber if we'd left Morocco and come to a new country."

She laughed quietly. "Although he was very annoyed with me, first he smiled, then he began to laugh, and he turned around — because, of course, I was walking behind him the way I thought a good wife should do — and he stopped the mule, put my bags on his shoulders, and made me ride on the animal's back.

"When we finally arrived at the bakery I asked why he'd wasted the mule on me, and he said that if I got lost in this 'new country,' he was afraid he'd never find me again! That was the moment I began to love him."

I tried to imagine Selina arriving for the first time in that very room.

"My husband was a gentle man, with a kind spirit, like Walid's. He never had a cruel word for his son or daughter, and he worked hard to give them a good life. He didn't always know what to make of his very intelligent children, but he loved them and let them make their own decisions. I think that's the best way a father can love his children. After all, the world is always changing, and we must give our children the best we can, then let them find their own wings, and fly."

"I wish you could have known my mother," I said softly.

"I do know her," Selina answered, "through you. I know she was a woman of great faith, gentleness and dignity. Those things she gave to you, along with her spirit and will to survive. You could not have come through so much without her."

Selina understood, without jealousy, my longing for my mother on the eve of my wedding.

"Your mother is here with you now," she said in a near-whisper. "I feel her just there, on your other side, holding your hand. She's smiling, because she knows how much you're loved. She's happy because she sees you're safe. She wants you to be at peace tonight. She is full of joy for you."

Now I was crying, and Selina took me in her arms and rocked me gently, singing a lullaby we both loved.

When she got up to leave, smoothing the covers over me, she said, "On the night before the wedding you should have a sponge to wipe out the past, a rose to make the present sweet, and a kiss to salute the future." She kissed my forehead. "Sleep well, my daughter."

Walid and I were married on my new birthday, March 15, 2013. In becoming his wife, I added his name to my mother's surname, becoming al-Maghribi Zahra Leila. Our two witnesses were Bennis Rachid and his wife, Bennis al-Maghribi Hania. Selina stood in the rear of the wedding salon, quieting her two grandsons, Tariq and baby Idir. The ceremony, performed by a deputy in the municipal office, was over in minutes. We then gathered on the steps outside the building, where Amin took photographs while his sisters showered us with rose petals.

In the photographs I'm wearing the crème silk dress, colorful silver earrings and a matching bracelet. My left hand bears a gold wedding band. My eyes are flawlessly lined with *khol* and my lips are soft pink. My bejeweled shoes peek from beneath my hem. I'm holding a bouquet of pink and yellow roses. I am more beautiful than I ever dreamed I could be.

Walid, in his dark suit, stands tall and straight beside me. Selina, in light blue, is on the other side. Hania and Rachid, behind us, hold their curly-headed sons. And Fatima and Aisha are close by, like my guardian angels.

I am surrounded by people who truly care about me. I have a family. My family loves me, and I love them, too.

After the wedding we all go to a restaurant on the waterfront, not far from the tearoom. The owner is one of our customers; he purchases our bread and offers my pastries as desserts for his wealthy diners. He has arranged for us to have a private room and a splendid meal: I love the round, musty taste of the *mrouzia tagine*, made with mutton, and the *saalouk* salad of eggplants, squash and peppers. I eat rice pudding while everyone claps, and the chef serves us his own *haloua rhifa*, which I know, from Selina's private wink, is not as good as mine.

Afterwards, the others kiss us, and wave as we climb into a taxi and drive along the waterfront to a gleaming hotel. When we arrive, a doorman escorts us directly to a glass elevator that looks out over the lobby as it climbs. I don't tell Walid I've never ridden in an elevator, nor even a taxi, before. I'm speechless when the doorman leads us into a room with windows offering both a view of the sea to the far horizon, and the nighttime city, now twinkling in the falling night.

And then we are alone.

I've had many weeks to prepare myself for this moment. I have fought to find the strength not to show Walid my fear. I know what must happen, and I secretly pray that I'll find a way to bear it, out of my love for my husband.

Walid and I stand, face to face. His eyes are tired, and though he is happy, sadness lingers behind his smile. He takes my hands. The new gold band feels heavy as his fingers clasp mine.

"Leila, I've been with no other woman since Nora. For many years even the thought of another woman has left me terribly afraid. I'm not sure I can be a husband to you in that way, quite yet. I'm asking you to give me time."

Though I believe him, I know he is thinking, first, of me.

That night he holds me in his arms. When we finally fall asleep, his body warm beside me, I almost feel safe. Almost.

7. THE KAFTAN

Our wedding night began in kindness and trust. Yet despite Walid's promise never to hurt me, I awoke before dawn, heart pounding, afraid that if I moved, the man in bed beside me might, like Young Master, suddenly become a stranger. I lay next to my new husband, a thin *kaftan* wrapped tightly around my body, nauseated with fear.

Walid's arm curled over my shoulders and his body cupped my back. His breathing, a warm sigh in my ear, sent prickly tremors down my spine and his hair, which I so often longed to touch, seemed to scour my neck.

I felt his height and weight surround me, not lovingly as it had the night before, but as a bird must feel when held in human hands. Fear poured through my body, causing the room to flutter and darken, even in the brightening of the day.

Slowly I shifted my left knee, hoping to lessen the pressure on my injured hip, and almost as if bound together, Walid moved, too. The arm wrapped around my shoulder slid away, but now his hand rested heavily on my thigh. My breathing grew shallower and I felt my forehead bead up with sweat. I could not imagine why I had agreed to marry anyone, let alone a man still haunted by his own ghosts.

Tears flooded my eyes and I pushed his arm aside, sliding to my feet and making my way in the semi-darkness to the bathroom. Securely locked inside, I sank to the floor, head buried in my arms.

Within moments I heard Walid's voice on the other side of the door. "Leila, are you alright?"

I wiped my tears and clenched my hands to stop them from shaking.

"I'm fine," I lied, praying he couldn't tell I was crying. Though I knew he wanted to, he did not attempt to open the door.

"My love," he said gently, "please come back to bed. I'll take a blanket and sleep on the floor."

"No — you mustn't sleep on the floor," I answered, bitterly ashamed that he understood me so well.

"You don't have to worry. I promised never to hurt you and I meant it."

I didn't respond.

"Leila —" Walid's voice had a growing urgency. "Please say something."

Still, I couldn't speak. How could I explain that every moment of my life was spent trying to find a way through the caverns of my fear? Fear of hunger. Fear of being beaten. Fear of the cold. Fear of men and fear of women. Fear of being recognized and returned to those who did not care whether I lived or died.

"Leila, please open the door."

How could I make him understand that I would *never* be able to open the door, because I had sealed the doors shut from anyone and anything that might hurt me?

His promise, though made with all his heart, meant nothing. I knew, because life had taught me well, that in an instant the world can twist like leaves in the wind, and those who once seemed to care for me were perfectly capable of taking pleasure in my agony.

Walid fell silent, waiting. Knowing, as I knew, that there would never be any end to my fear. He could protect me from some things, perhaps even protect me from himself. But no one, and nothing, could protect me from my fear.

I heard him sit on the other side of the door, unable, or unwilling to move. He was prepared to remain there until I was willing — and able — to return to him.

Minutes passed, and my heart grew still. I felt heavy, exhausted, empty. The silence from the other room seemed to beckon, for I knew I couldn't remain locked away forever.

Slowly I got to my feet. I took a deep breath. I unlocked the door. Walid sat in a position that mirrored mine, his head in his hands. He looked up, a question in his troubled eyes.

"You've done nothing to cause this," I said.

"Yes, I did," he replied. "I didn't understand how difficult this would be for you."

"No, Walid," I whispered. "I must —"

"—There's nothing you *must* do," he said, also climbing to his feet.

His eyes met mine, and suddenly I understood: *he was afraid, too*. Despite having been loved all his life by his family; despite having a home, enough to eat, the chance to study, fall in love and marry the woman he loved — he, too, knew how quickly the world can be swallowed by endless night.

"Memory is a burden," I murmured, echoing the words Bahia had said to me long before. 'It's a weight that none of us can afford to carry."

"Yet we can't be free of it," Walid replied. He held out his hands. "I didn't mean to frighten you this morning. I will try to be more careful in the future."

"And I'll try," I answered, "to find the strength not to be ruled by my past."

After that first morning of our married life, Walid and I reached a kind of truce, as if, in exhaustion, we decided not to wage a war against our pasts anymore.

We lived together as the closest of friends — two people who expressed their love in shared solitude. Neither felt the need to say more than was necessary; we often found we were thinking the same thing at the same moment. His feelings were clear to me at a glance; my feelings were clear to him, even when I didn't meet his eyes.

We slept together, and his arms were protective. Though I awakened sometimes in the night, bathed in sweat and trembling, I knew Walid was not Young Master. And when he grew silent and stared for long moments into the distance, I knew he was making peace with a memory, and was not unhappy with me.

For some months our lives continued in this rhythm. I began learning the basic elements of written French. Fatima offered to speak nothing but French with me. Amin selected novels by famous French authors for me to read. "You may find this peculiar," he said of *The Stranger*, but it offers a fascinating view of the sickness of those who feel no responsibility to anyone but themselves."

"I see Amin has given you another of his favorites," Walid remarked, lifting his bulging shoulder bag. "Well, my father always said that a book is a garden in one's pocket."

We often had dinner with Hania and Rachid, who, with two children, now rarely left home in the evenings. Neither Hania nor Selina ever teased us about the flatness of my belly, or why we were never tired when we rose before dawn. The peace we created was more valuable than waging war against the pain hiding just beneath the surface of our lives.

If this was the happiness we crafted for ourselves, who could say it was less than our own perfect love?

A nd then, one evening I stepped out of my bath just as Walid walked into the bathroom. Though I had stopped locking the door, it was our habit to keep a respectful distance when undressed.

Walid looked up in surprise. "Leila, please excuse me. I didn't realize you were here."

"Of course," I said shyly as I reached for my *kaftan*, hanging on a hook on the door. Though Walid had seen my scarred shoulders when I was sleeveless in the heat of our kitchen, no one but Hania had seen my maimed body. Now he turned away and removed the *kaftan*, holding it politely toward me without looking in my direction.

I brought the robe up to my body as he grasped the doorknob, and called him quietly. He paused, his gaze still turned away.

"Walid," I said quietly, "please look at me."

Years later I would recall how still Walid became. I remember his posture: always restrained, somewhat tense, ever watchful, like a cat fully aware of its surroundings, even when it appeared to be asleep.

At that moment Walid weighed whether to risk the delicate balance we had put in place on that first morning of our married life. He feared that responding to my words might make me once again a prisoner of my memories. Though our life together was different from the lives of others, it was a life filled with caring.

I, too, did not fully understand why I'd spoken those words. Then, in a flash of insight that might have come from god, I realized that *I could no longer bear the solitude of my flesh.*

I could no longer live in the prison of my scars.

I needed, if only at that moment, to feel the touch of another human being.

I didn't know what would happen later. I couldn't guess what ghosts would come howling in the night to punish me for taking this risk.

I only knew, with every cell, every sense, with each of my heartbeats, that I needed to form a blood-trust with the man I loved.

Walid turned his head slowly enough to allow me to reconsider. It seemed an eternity before his eyes found mine. I saw that he was still grasping the door, as if he, too, might need to flee. I saw *his* fear, for himself, and for me.

But he waited. He waited until the *kaftan* drifted soundlessly to the floor.

We recreated the world that night.

Slowly, with indescribable tenderness, patience and love.

I hadn't dreamed that my skin could sing from the mere tip of a finger. Or that the brush of his tongue could ignite a fire in my belly. I didn't know that a kiss had a language all its own, or so much could be shared without a word.

When the past crowded in and my body tensed, Walid murmured, "look at me, Leila. Don't close your eyes."

And when he paused, silenced by his grief, I took his face in my hands and pressed my lips against his.

Though it was far from easy, and there were tears from us both, we found our way to an aching pleasure, and knew that pleasure would be easier for us both, in time.

Much later, in the darkness, I was moved to speak. In a voice as calm as the wind at dusk I told him about my family, the house of pleasure, and finally, the home of the judge. I also spoke of Young Master, though when I tried to recall the worst parts of those nights, I found that much was swept away. My tormentor's face was strangely blurred, his voice more a thought than a sound. Though I wanted to release this burden, I found that I could not. My mind blocked my memory in the way that steel doors protect a vault.

Still, more than once Walid make a choking noise as he listened. Then he held me, singing softly, until we both fell into untroubled sleep.

For some months we lived in this way, our lives bound by hard work and intense pleasure, our family and friends close beside us.

All was well, until the day of the *amandines*.

8. Amandines

January 29, 2014

13:33 p.m.

Perhaps it is true that the taller the castle, the closer the lightening.

Idir was asleep in his crib in the cupboard behind the tearoom. The little space, sometimes used for storing extra flour or bags of sugar, always smelled like the warm, sweet breath of a breast-fed baby. Tariq, too old for afternoon naps, colored pictures at the worktable, while Aliah and Shada's quick hands kneaded a large mound of dough. We were baking *amandines,* a marzipan-filled pastry that had become our most popular sweet.

We'd heard on the radio that a group of government officials' wives, visiting Casablanca from Rabat, would be touring the waterfront that morning, and we'd worked hard to prepare for their visit.

Hania had taken Selina to the eye doctor, despite her furious complaints that our vendors' invoices were written in ever-smaller print, and her eyes were just fine.

Walid had gone to the bank to make a payment on our lease. The tearoom was doing so well, we'd decided to make additional payments and to extend our lease, fearing the landlord might raise the rent. I knew Walid would be away for several hours, but felt little concern. With Shada and Aliah in the kitchen to assist me, I expected the day to go well, like any other.

The afternoon was stormy: a flag on the building across the street snapped red and green, and waves spat foam high above the seawall. The clouds strewn along the horizon shone purple against the roiling sky. Even the gulls wheeled loosely over the empty beach, their cries shrill and plaintive in the winter sun.

The first woman was clad in leather so soft it folded like butter over her belt. Her black knit skirt fell short of her ankles, so one could see her boots matched her jacket. Her headscarf, held in place with bejeweled pins, was wrapped multiple times, French style, around her neck. She shouldered a purse I'd seen in Hania's magazines, and wore enormous dark glasses.

She entered noisily and threw back her head in a laugh that trumpeted throughout the tearoom. Behind her came several other women in traditional blue *djellabas*, except the fabric was embossed with the symbols of Parisian designers. They, too, wore gold-rimmed sunglasses that covered much of their faces. Their laughter, though not as loud, was sarcastic, as if mocking something they'd seen in the street. All carried bags from expensive waterfront boutiques.

The last two women, clearly younger, made a curious pair. The taller of the two wore a *burka* that covered everything but her eyes. Her black robes swept the floor and her hands vanished in hidden pockets. I only knew she was young by the extended slash of her eyeliner. I wondered how she came to be with the others, especially when compared to the woman standing beside her.

Only slightly taller than me, her slender form was framed by her thin white *djellaba*, an odd choice for the January weather. Her hair, which most likely had been entirely hidden by her headscarf before she went out in the wind, was pure blonde. High cheekbones, a fine nose and lips made her indistinguishable from the European tourists, and she wore make-up to draw attention to her wide, sky-blue eyes. Turning toward the counter, she reached up to adjust her scarf, and I had a moment to study her.

Her hair, unusually heavy for its color and texture, was swept back and clasped in a glittering, sapphire-studded barrette. My fingers tightened on the edge of the counter. I knew that barrette. I had polished it many times.

Aware of her beauty, she glanced around the room to see who was watching, eyes resting for an instant on the faces of men and women alike.

Then her eyes found mine.

A sudden prickling raced along my shoulders to the small of my back.

She blinked and drew her brows together before her expression shifted to disbelief, hands frozen on the edges of her sheer white scarf.

At the same instant, the leather jacket led the group to the display cases, where she exalted our pastries in a mixture of Arabic — tinged with the accent of Rabat — and French. I realized that these were the visitors from the capital, and the younger women, most likely from provincial cities, had joined them on this excursion to Casablanca. I now understood why my Young Mistress was dressed so strangely: she did not have access to such stores in the *souk* of Essaouira to compete with these women.

Aliah appeared from the kitchen with a tray of warm *amandines,* and placed them in the display cases. The woman in leather trilled at the sight of the fresh pastries, wondering whether "one might find true French cuisine in Casablanca." Barely looking at me, she asked if they might try a sample.

I removed several *amandines, pain au raisons, milles feuilles* and chocolate *éclairs* from the case, cut each pastry into small sections and set the array on a serving dish. All the women, save Young Mistress, helped themselves. Young Mistress had barely moved. Her eyes were fixed on me.

The leather jacket now ordered food and drinks for the group. I fetched the pastries, aware of Young Mistress' blue gaze, and turned to prepare the tea. The women selected a table near the windows and moved as if in a herd, all the time speaking loudly. They never removed their sunglasses.

Young Mistress, however, drew closer to the counter. As I lifted the tray she tilted her head, scrutinizing my hair, covered with a mauve scarf. She took in my green eyes. She studied, with particular intensity, my scar.

Straightening my back, I walked past her, amazed that my hands weren't shaking, and served the other women. When I returned, she was waiting.

"Madame?" I asked as I regained my place behind the counter. My voice was calm. Pleasant. Professional.

"Where are you from?" she asked in French.

I smiled politely. "One doesn't have to be born in Paris to make fine French pastry. Please try an *amandine*. People say ours are the best in Casablanca."

Confused, she glanced away for a moment, unable to match the woman standing before her with the starving, trembling girl who'd served her years before. Her eyes fell to my hands. She stared for a moment at my wedding ring, then eyed the quality of my *djellaba*.

"Your French is quite good," she said belligerently.

"Madame is too generous."

"Did you learn it here?"

"I studied French in school, like most Moroccans."

"But you have a Parisian accent."

"My professor would be very proud."

Once again uncertainty swept her face. She was well aware how unseemly it was for a woman of her class to ask personal questions of a shop girl — even moreso, when in the company of other officials' wives.

"But are you from Casablanca?" she now asked in Arabic, her voice low.

"Madame?" I replied, expressing mock surprise.

"Where were you born?" she insisted, leaning closer to the glass.

"My family has always lived here," I answered in Arabic. "Why do you ask?"

"You — you remind me of someone from Essaouira."

"I have no friends in Essaouira," I replied in a pleasant voice.

"How long have you worked in this tearoom?"

"I've been here since it opened."

"What was your job before you worked here?"

"I worked in a different bakery."

"Where were you trained to bake?"

"I learned how to make our famous *amandines* here in Casablanca."

"But you —" she was interrupted by the woman in the leather jacket.

"*Ma cherie*! Have you fallen in love with the pastries? Come join us! Your tea is getting cold!"

Young Mistress sat down with the others, but placed herself so she could watch me work. I went back to arranging the food, wiping counters and refilling the samovar. Their voices carried shrilly over the other customers, so I listened without appearing to do so.

The women spoke in Arabic punctuated with French phrases and expressions, including the names of streets and fashion houses. They discussed the Galleries Lafayette, a store I'd seen in many of Hania's magazines, as if they shopped there regularly. One woman complained about the long lines to enter the Longchamps boutique (*"It is always overrun with Japanese tourists!"*), but added that the selection of perfumes justified the trouble (*"Where else can you buy authentic Hermès, as well as the newest Guerlain in one trip?"*). Another claimed her husband purchased her formal jewelry only in Monte Carlo, because the streets near the casino had the world's best selection of uncut gemstones, which were then set by their personal goldsmith in Zürich. The third said her husband only shopped for her when traveling in Amsterdam, because the Jewish merchants sold diamonds brought directly from South Africa. Young Mistress and the woman in the *burka* said nothing at all.

Suddenly one of the women asked Young Mistress what it was like to live in a city as small as Essaouira. I heard her stammer a reply about the long history of her husband's family, and how important it was to maintain their influence in the city of their ancestors.

"My husband's house is one of the oldest in Essaouira, and is actually built into the ancient city walls," she continued loudly. "You can hear the sea from every room, and there are absolutely splendid views of the Atlantic from the terrace on the roof. The house is so large I haven't yet seen all the rooms, and we need live-in servants to maintain it. Of course, it's extremely difficult to find staff who don't damage the property, or steal. They simply have no respect for our way of life."

I willed myself to react to nothing. Walking into the kitchen, I leaned against the wall, breathing deeply. Should

I simply leave through the rear door and escape along the beach? I knew Young Mistress wasn't entirely sure I was the girl they'd been hunting for years, and neither Shada nor Aliah would be able to answer her questions, for they knew nothing of my past.

But to leave would confirm her suspicions, bringing down the wrath of my Master against Walid and Selina. No, I decided, I would continue to play the role of the confident shopkeeper, and pray she wouldn't guess the truth.

Lifting another tray of pastries, I calmly returned to the display cases. The conversation at the wives' table had turned to the advantages of living in Rabat.

"One thing is certain," an older woman said. "When my husband travels, I'm always pleased to be living in the capital. The presence of the royal family virtually insures the city is safe. One hears so much about lax security in the rest of the country."

"How true!" another exclaimed. "The situation is terrible in Marrakech. With so many wealthy Europeans purchasing homes, then leaving them empty for months at a time, we all live under the constant threat of robbery. We'll be in Turkey for eight weeks this spring, so we plan to hire two additional guards to protect our property." The woman addressed Young Mistress.

"How are you doing without your husband, Sabrina? He's been away for quite a while."

Five faces turned in her direction.

"I — I receive many visits from friends, and my family, of course, when Nassim's away," she answered, shifting her gaze from me.

"Do you also employ guards?"

"Yes, at night," she replied evasively.

"Be sure you also have someone good in the kitchen," the oldest said. "You can always find servants to clean, but next to security, there's nothing in the world as important as a talented cook."

"Particularly if you entertain," leather jacket said.

"And you need a good seamstress," the oldest woman continued. "It's better to spend a bit more and have your clothes personally made," she added with a glance at Young Mistress' thin *djellaba*. "Nothing they sell in the souk is worth the money. These days most of it's imported from China."

"So tell us," leather jacket said, "where has your handsome husband been posted this time?"

"Canada," Young Mistress answered proudly. "He's been named assistant vice-consul in our diplomatic offices in Montreal and Vancouver."

"Montreal and Vancouver? And he didn't take you with him?"

All the women burst into laughter, and Young Mistress' face tightened.

"You could have perfected your English!" one said.

"Yes, and you'd have been close enough to New York and Los Angeles to shop!" another agreed.

"*Habiba*, you must *always* accompany your husband when he's posted to a desirable place," the oldest woman said, "especially if the appointment is for an extended period. How long will he be away?"

"Two years," Young Mistress said, "but he's already served seven months, and of course he visits regularly."

"Montreal is absolutely horrid in winter," one woman exclaimed, "but the summers are charming. I have a brother who's lived there for years. Two of his sons attended medical school at McGill."

"Vancouver is quite pleasant as well," said the older woman, "though it rains a bit too much for my taste. It's rather like London or Zurich in the spring. But you really must visit him, Sabrina. Husbands do best when they're not left alone too long."

I glanced up to see knowing looks exchanged between the women.

"It's perfectly alright —" leather jacket reassured the group. "Nassim's travels provide our young friend here the perfect excuse to come to the big city more often."

"How true," another woman exclaimed. "After living in France, I don't see how you can stand Essaouira. Didn't you attend university in Paris?"

"Yes, I studied —"

"Well, you should spend as much time as possible in Rabat. We have the finest stores in Morocco, without having to be bothered with tourists. And, of course, your father-in-law now lives in Rabat, too. I'm sure he wouldn't object to your escaping Essaouira from time to time."

Young Mistress lowered her eyes and I continued with my work.

Eventually the women rose, collecting their shopping bags. Young Mistress stood, too, her eyes once again seeking my face. I kept my attention on organizing receipts at the cash register.

The group moved to the door, still speaking loudly. Just as they reached the threshold young Tariq, followed by baby Idir, came out of the kitchen and ran straight to me. As was his habit, Tariq, whose dark curly hair and melting brown eyes belonged to his mother, threw his arms around my waist and buried his face in my apron. Idir, still sleepy-eyed from his nap, bounced over and raised his arms. I bent low, swept him up and set him on my stronger hip.

"Hello, little men!" I said in Berber. "Are you hungry?"

There was a noise by the door. The three of us looked up to find Young Mistress standing at the threshold, white-faced, fingers over her mouth.

Her blue gaze was fixed on Tariq. The other women immediately surrounded her, asking whether she might be ill. I set Idir down slowly and told Tariq to take his brother into the kitchen and wait for me there. Hearing the tension in my voice, he did so without complaint,.

Now, though we stood on opposite sides of the tearoom, I saw in Young Mistress' face that her marriage to Young Master had borne no fruit. I knew that, having given birth to no children, her belief that a servant girl from the distant mountains should have not one son, but *two*, was more than she could bear.

After a few moments she squared her shoulders and drew in a deep, long breath. I saw a promise, passed wordlessly from her gaze to mine, that she would make me pay, not only for escaping their control, but also — though she was sadly mistaken — for managing to accomplish what she had not.

She believed I had become a mother.

9. THIEF

JANUARY 29TH, 2014

17:11

The police truck had blackened windows and black seats. Two officers climbed in front; the other two sat in the rear, on either side of me. I didn't look back, because I couldn't bear to take with me the faces of Shada and Aliah, who watched from the doorway in speechless disbelief. Yet I couldn't close my eyes, because some part of me knew it might be many months before I would again see the white gulls swirling the reddened evening sands, or the smooth cement walls, colorful with graffiti, rising along the sea.

I couldn't allow my thoughts to turn to what Hania and Selina, but most of all, Walid, would feel when they learned of my arrest. No, I would not think of that, now. Instead, I emptied my face of all emotion, as I had learned many years ago, and kept my gaze focused on the shoulders of the men in the front. My body could be taken, but I would not let them take my soul. That, I had also learned since the last time I'd been enslaved.

They slammed the doors and the outside world abruptly vanished, except for a rectangle of darkening sky, visible through the windshield. No one could see in. I could barely see out. Strange, how easily the world could be stolen!

Whenever I saw a police car I always thought of the first time I'd tried to escape from Essaouira, with a young man whose kindness had nearly caused his own arrest. That time I'd been too frightened to take much notice of the vehicle. Now I was acutely aware of every detail of the journey.

I expected the truck to stink of those who drank wine until, drenched with vomit and sweat, they staggered through the souk and lay muttering in doorways. I believed police vehicles were soiled with the mud of thieves who fled from the old people and young mothers they'd robbed. I even thought I might catch a trace of the hashish prized by so many, and yet the source of despair in other's lives.

The truck might, I believed, be fouled by the excrement of fear, the mucous of tears, the stink of fallen women, and the metallic residue of guilty blood. Instead, it held the acrid smell of newly tanned leather, an odor that brought back my earliest childhood, and the brine of stale sweat mixed with cheap cologne.

A metal grill separated the back seat from the front, and I felt a strange desire to lift my hands and lace my fingers through the holes, as I had grasped the grill on the window when I sang in the blind woman's chamber. Perhaps I needed to add touch to the sight, sound and scent of my imprisonment. I feared, however, that raising my arms would give my captors reason to claim I was violent, or treacherous, or tried to escape, so I kept still. I found it quite easy to see myself as they saw me. After all, this was one skill every victim needed in order to survive.

Abruptly we pulled away from the curb and made a sharp turn, spitting sand and splinters of broken glass onto the sidewalk. The officer in the front passenger seat responded to the sudden growl of the radio by identifying himself and announcing in a loud voice that the suspect had been apprehended. The *suspect?* Was he speaking of *me?*

We drove along the seafront, the beaches nearly empty. Within an hour, as darkness shrouded the water, strings of colored lights and neon signs would beckon people to sit on the beachside terraces. Men would gather around outdoor televisions to cheer on their favorite football teams, while the women gossiped, one eye on the children chasing each other on the cool, damp sand.

"Well, this wasn't difficult," the policeman in the front seat remarked. "I'd say ten minutes, in and out."

"I'm glad about that," the driver agreed, lighting a cigarette. "I'm off in thirty minutes and my wife complains about me being late all the time."

"Shit. After everything we heard, I expected she'd be wearing a bomb belt or packing a SIG! What the hell? I'll bet she couldn't handle a kitchen knife!"

The officer on my left laughed and observed me coolly. "What do you suppose she *really* did? I don't believe that stuff in the report." He pressed his thigh against mine.

"I don't know, but I'm sure he enjoyed it," the driver answered, gazing at me in the rearview mirror. "She's not too bad if you ignore the scar."

"Only if you're into kids," the man on my right replied. "She looks like she's about twelve. And I'm pretty sure she doesn't have anything worth looking at underneath that robe."

They all laughed and the images rose before my eyes, even as I struggled to blink them away: A rainy night many years before. The rear of a black, rusting truck. Low male voices in the darkness. Words about the girl crouched in the narrow space behind the seats.

Their laughter blended with the laughter of the guests at the brothel, where I was forced to sing for men who looked at me with hungry eyes. The laughter of my Young

Master as I bore his weight, battered by his hips. The laughter of the men in the streets of Casablanca when I begged for scraps to keep from starving.

A tear loosened itself and coursed down my cheek, splashing silently onto my wrists. *Do not let them see you cry*, I entreated myself. *Do. Not. Cry!*

The wind sent fronds of palm trees into a frenzied dance as we passed the gates of the port and turned into the tangled streets of the old city. Cars jockeyed for space in the crush of slow-moving traffic, as men and women wearily wound their way home from work.

"Why don't you turn on the air-conditioning?" the man to my right complained, wiping sweat from beneath his beret. The man to my left shifted slightly; his upper arm pressed my breast. He moved it carefully back and forth, searching for my nipple. I kept my eyes focused on the rectangle of sky.

Fiddling with the knobs, the driver smacked the dashboard with the palm of his hand. "It doesn't work!"

"Then start the siren, idiot! Do you want to be here all night?"

Traffic slowly parted, making way for our bleating vehicle. I could see the flashing red and blue lights reflected in shop windows, as customers and school children turned and stared.

It took a long time to make our way through the center of the city, past the gritty streets of concrete apartment blocks, markets brimming with late shoppers, and the winding white passages of the old quarter. In the distance I heard the *muezzin* calling the faithful to evening prayer.

Then, as we picked up speed and the faces of people on the streets softened to a blur, I wondered whether Selina would regret I'd ever crossed their doorway. After all, Walid had only begun to make peace with his past. What would become of them now?

17:53

The naked cement building was like a face without eyes, the doors a gaping mouth that closed tight behind us. I was taken through a narrow passage into a hall, where the hot flow of rusting fans stirred stacks of papers on gunmetal desks. The hall echoed with ringing telephones and men talking loudly. All looked at me curiously, unused to what appeared to be a child, surrounded by officers.

I was led down a steep staircase to a passage that stank of decaying plaster, and into a small grey cell containing only a wooden stool. They took my wedding ring, bag, and shoes. I sank down on the stool and faced the narrow beam of light shining through a slot in the door. From time to time someone passed the slot and looked inside. The heat was so intense, I struggled to breathe. I needed to urinate, and felt a thirst as wide as the Sahara.

It seemed I waited for hours. I could hear nothing in the corridors, and was offered no food or drink. I did my best not to dwell on what happened the last time I'd been in police custody. The scars beneath my robe began to prickle, and my fingers stole to the thick scar beneath my left eye.

Rising, I walked in slow steps around the cell, measuring two paces forward and back. I could touch all four walls simply by stretching out my arms. Had the ceiling not been so high I might have passed out for lack of air.

Still, my senses dulled with the crawling minutes, and soon I was no longer one with my flesh.

I remembered this feeling, too: it had happened when Hassan beat me, or whenever Young Master came into my room at night. I had watched from a foggy distance, yet I felt nothing, no matter how badly they hurt me. The pain came later, when I was alone, waiting for the dawn.

Now Selina's voice flittered through my mind, and I murmured the words along with her: *"Love of my heart, how can I find you? Day of my life, how can I use you? I reach for the sky; I trust in the earth, I sing heaven's song, I am filled with your —*

The door banged open and a woman dressed in a black robe, face shadowed by the hood, stood at the threshold.

"Come. Now."

"Please. I need a toilet."

Silence.

"Please. Where is a toilet?"

She grasped my arm and walked me down a corridor, past many doors. At the end of the hall she turned into a room with a table and three orange plastic chairs. The walls were painted an intense blue-green, and the florescent light suspended over the table gave everything a sickly yellowish hue.

"Please —"

She pointed to a chair facing a mirror on the opposite wall, then left, shutting the door behind her.

I sank down and folded my hands in my lap to keep them from trembling. The room seemed to shift. I feared my bladder might explode.

For many more minutes, I waited. Sweat drenched my body beneath my robes, and I was ashamed that I would begin to stink. After what seemed like yet another hour, the door opened and two men in white shirts and dark pants came into the room. The older, who was smoking a cigarette, measured me with sharp black eyes while the younger, whose shirt was stained with great rings at the armpits, dropped a folder, a pad of paper and a pen on the table.

They seated themselves on either side of me, scraping the chairs along the cement floor. Despite my fear of appearing to be weak, I lowered my eyes respectfully, hoping they wouldn't take this as a sign of guilt.

"Good evening, Madame," the older man said in a measured voice. We've spent some time looking though our records. It seems you didn't exist until a few months ago."

I didn't answer. They waited. The younger man spoke. "Please explain this."

"I — I don't know."

"Why don't you begin by telling us where you come from."

I pushed my trembling hands deeper into the folds of my robe. "I come from a village in the mountains above Marrakech."

He wrote on his paper. "What year were you born?"

"I don't know."

"You don't know?"

"My mother and father could not read or write, and I left them when I was very young."

"Are your parents dead?"

"I don't know."

"Where are they, now?"

"I don't know."

"When was the last time you saw them?"

"The night I was — the night I left."

"When was that?"

"I don't know."

"Was it last month? Last year? Five years ago?"

"Many years ago. I don't know the exact date."

"What are their names?"

I paused to buy myself time to make up names for my mother and father. Though it was dangerous, I was even more afraid to tell him more than was absolutely necessary.

The younger officer drew his chair a few inches closer and stared hard into my face. "We're waiting."

"My father's name was Mohammed. Mohammed Tahrir. And my mother —"

"Madame," he cut in, "I don't believe you."

There was nothing I could say. He waited through my silence, then asked why I'd left my family.

"I — I went away to work."

"Where?"

"To Essaouira."

"Why?"

"My father could no longer feed me."

"How old were you?"

"I was about twelve."

"Twelve? How could a twelve year old get from Marrakech to Essaouira?" He looked at the other officer, who snorted disbelievingly.

"I was taken there by —" I paused, struggling to keep my voice from shaking — "by some men who knew my father."

There was another silence. I felt their eyes on me, lingering on the good quality of my *djellaba*, the unusual colors of my eyes and skin, the texture of my hair. Like many people in my world, they wondered whether I was Berber or Arab. They wondered how I, with my child's body and broken face, came to work in the seaside tearoom. They wondered how a woman born in a backward mountain village survived in their modern city.

They believed I was lying.

"Were these men who took you to Essaouira members of your family?"

I shook my head.

"No father sends his daughter away with strangers."

I did not respond.

"You're telling us your father allowed you to travel to a distant city to work at such a young age?"

"Many children must work to eat," I answered quietly.

They paused. The truth was in my accent, which even after many years, still bore the inflections of my impoverished birth.

"Where did you work in Essaouira?" the older man asked.

"In the home of a woman," I answered.

"What was her name?"

"I knew her only as 'Mistress.'"

"And you lived with her until you came to Casablanca?"

"No," I said, my heart speeding up, even as I tried to remain calm. "I worked for someone else when I was older."

"And what was that person's name?"

I hesitated. In truth, I had spoken my former master's name only twice since escaping.

"You already know," I answered, softly.

"It is true, then, that you were the servant of the Minister of Justice?"

I paused, confused. "I — I was the servant of a judge."

"But that judge has since been named Minister of Justice in the government of our King."

Astonished, I looked up. The man stared back with steel in his eyes. "So you admit you resided in the home of the Minister?"

I shook my head. "I lived in Essaouira, but —"

"And you left his home six years ago?"

"I don't know exactly when I left."

"But you departed without his permission?"

"I — I don't believe I need permission to leave any home except that of my father or husband."

"Then you are going to pretend you don't know why you've been arrested?"

"Have I been arrested?" I asked, summoning all my courage to continue to look in his eyes. "I have not been made aware of any charges against me."

For a long moment, there was no sound.

"Perhaps," he said without releasing my gaze, "I should tell you that you have been sought for some time."

"What crime am I accused of?"

"Theft," he answered, his eyes once again traveling the length of my body, as if he believed I was hiding stolen goods beneath my robe.

"Theft?" I echoed, praying my fear was not revealed in my voice. "I came to Casablanca with nothing, and now live as a simple baker. What could I have stolen to make me so valuable to a Minister?"

I saw rage leap into his eyes.

"I do not question the wisdom of those who run our nation. If the Minister says you are a thief, then it is true. I *do* see that you are cunning, as he wrote in his description. But rest assured — we will get the truth — all of it. Your days of evading justice are over."

"I didn't know my Master as a Minister," I said wearily, "and although I lived in his home for some years, I saw him only a few times."

The older officer finished his cigarette. He ground the butt into the floor with the toe of his shoe and sighed.

"To be honest," he said, "we have more important things to do than to sit here, listening to your lies. Many matters in this city are far more deserving of our attention. We need to take care of this matter quickly and get back to our real work. So why don't you simply tell us what you did and why you did it?"

"I haven't committed any crimes."

"Please don't try my patience," he said in an unnaturally calm voice. I recognized that voice, having heard it used by men throughout my life. I knew that very soon he would allow the younger man to hurt me.

"I'm not lying," I said quietly.

The younger officer leaned in closer. "Do you deny that you are Senhaji Rana, who at other times have gone by the name of Hagar?"

"I am al-Maghribi Zahra Leila."

"You told the officers earlier you've also been known by those other names."

"I have been called other things, but my name is al-Maghribi Zahra Leila."

The older man spoke.

"You took a number of personal possessions from your employer, his mother and his son's wife when you *chose* to leave."

"What?" A current of fear shot through me. He looked back coldly.

"I see we're getting closer to the truth."

"I — I promise you, I took nothing when I left Essaouira," I stammered.

"But you informed them you were leaving."

"My young master and mistress had gone to Rabat."

"Which gave you plenty of opportunity to remove their belongings."

"I would never have —"

"And you took a leather bag filled with valuable possessions."

"I took nothing but the clothes on my back."

"These were *your* clothes?"

"They were the clothes I was wearing."

"Including several rings that had belonged to the Senhaji family for generations, and were given to your mistress on her wedding day!"

"Rings?" I stammered, "I know nothing about——"

"And a bracelet of such value it can never be replaced."

"A bracelet?"

"And this is why you fled Essaouira," he said, his voice still much too calm.

"We understand you had help from two sisters who ran a so-called 'Women's Center' in the souk, but were secretly helping servants to steal from their employers, then flee to larger cities, where the stolen articles were sold."

Now I felt my heart might leap from my chest. "*No!*" I cried. "I stole nothing from my employer and had help from no one when I left!"

"Yet you knew these women."

"What women?"

"The sisters who ran this Women's Center." He nearly spat the last two words.

"I did nothing criminal when I lived in Essaouira."

"Yet police records indicate you were arrested, while trying to leave the city with an unnamed man."

Tears flooded my eyes. "I became lost in the *souk* and feared my master's anger."

"So you tried to leave with a stranger?"

"I had no money for the bus."

"You were also accused of theft on that occasion," he remarked, picking up the folder and glancing at the papers inside. "I see the Minister was kind enough to drop the charge after you were released into his custody."

"I stole nothing. He claimed I was a thief so the police would look for me."

"A judge has no need to lie when he requests our assistance."

"Perhaps he was simply mistaken."

Both men stared as I fought back a sob. The younger spoke quietly.

"If a servant of mine was to steal, I would make sure she was appropriately punished. Perhaps the Minister was too lenient with you."

Unconsciously my hands stole to my face, now wet with tears.

"So, how did you find your way to Casablanca?" he continued. "It would seem rather too far to walk."

"I — I rode in a car."

"Whose car?"

"I don't know. They were strangers — tourists. I don't remember their names."

"Of course not."

"They spoke German. I believe they were newly married and —"

"You're making this up," the older man said.

"No — it's true. I approached them on the beach and they agreed to bring me here."

"I suppose you spoke to them in German."

"No, but they understood I wanted to leave, and they let me sit in their car."

"How did you pay them?"

"They wanted no pay."

"So you did not offer them the Minister's belongings?"

"I never touched my Master's things." Sweat, mixed with tears, now dripped down my face.

The two men exchanged glances. The younger wrote once more on the pad of paper. There was another long pause.

The older man again lit a cigarette, then casually tossed the still-burning match on the floor, close to the hem of my *djellaba*.

"You seem upset," he remarked, leaning back in his chair. "If you're telling the truth, you have nothing to fear."

He drew in and exhaled a long stream of smoke, stinging my eyes. I reached up with trembling fingers to wipe my face.

"So why was it so important for you to come to Casablanca? Did you think it would be easier to sell the jewelry?"

"I — I did not choose to come to Casablanca," I said, controlling my voice with difficulty. "I was only a passenger with people who were coming here."

"But if you stole nothing, why did you leave Essaouira?"

"I had been in my employer's house for many years, and I wanted a different life."

"Why would you be unhappy in the home of a judge?" the younger man interjected. "Weren't you given food to eat?

"Yes."

"Didn't he offer you clothes to wear and a place to sleep?"

I nodded.

"Didn't you learn to prepare food and care for a home while working for the Minister? Many would be glad to work in the home of such an important man."

"Yes, but —"

"You repaid his kindness by stealing from him."

"No, I —"

"Where is the jewelry now?"

"I didn't take it!"

"Where is the jewelry now?"

"I don't know —"

"What did you do with it?"

"I never took —"

The blow came so fast that when he struck me the world exploded into darkness. The plastic chair tipped over and my head struck the wall before I hit the floor. I heard a sickening crunch as I landed on my hip, and pain tore through my left shoulder. I threw up my arm to shield my face. He kicked me hard in the ribs.

"You make me sick, you lying bitch. We don't have time to listen to any more of your crap."

It was impossible to breathe. I coughed to clear my throat and tasted blood. Something warm poured from both my ear and temple. When I wiped my head, my sleeve was soaked dark red. My head ached as though struck with a hammer.

"Why don't you just confess?" the older officer said.

The stink of hot urine, mixed with sweat and blood, filled the room. Leaning forward, I retched bloody vomit on the front of my robe and it splattered to the floor.

The older man shook his head in disgust, stood up, and turned to the younger. "Get someone to clean this up."

He left, and the younger man stood over me, face twisted with contempt. "I'll bet you thought he'd never find you," he said quietly. "Stupid, stupid cow. Did you really think you could get away?"

❦ ❦ ❦

I awoke in a different cell.

I had no idea how much time had passed.

There was no light but for the thin strip of white beneath the door.

My entire body was on fire.

Though an unpainted metal shelf was bolted to the chipped wall, I was curled in a corner on the filthy floor, one arm around my head, the other holding my belly.

Slowly, carefully I stretched my legs, feeling a new, stabbing pain in my left hip, right shoulder and the ribs just below my heart. My face, swollen along the cheek where the officer struck me, was numb. Carefully I rolled into a sitting position. Leaning back against the wall, I realized that raising my chin so I faced the ceiling helped me breathe. I managed not to cry out, but tears flowed from my eyes and my mouth filled with the taste of sour milk and blood.

Despite the dim light I could make out a rusted metal sink and a stinking bucket in the opposite corner. I rolled over and crawled to the sink, praying the faucet worked. Using it for balance, I pulled myself to my feet and rested the right side of my body against the wall. My head ached as if I'd been struck with a club. I had no idea whether it was night or day, and I couldn't remember how I came to be there.

One handle on the faucet was broken, but the other groaned out a thin stream of brown water. I filled my hands and drank, then wet my soiled headscarf and wrapped it slowly around my head and face to soothe my swollen cheek. Though warm, the wet fabric felt like a balm.

Listening intently to the silence beyond the cell, I pulled off my *djellaba* with shaking hands and examined the purple flesh on my ribs and left hip. I poured water down my shoulders, grimacing, and did what I could to clean the dried blood, urine and vomit first from my body, then my robe.

Pinpricks of light danced before my eyes, so I leaned over the sink and focused on the thread of liquid draining from the spigot. My thoughts floated to the public fountain in the village of my childhood, where each morning the women gathered to complain about their husbands, their hunger, their lives.

The sound of bolts sliding on the door sent me scrambling to get my *djellaba* over my head. The door clanked open just as I pulled the hem over my hips, and I painfully slid my arms into the sleeves as light flooded the cell. The effort made my head spin, so I grasped the edge of the sink to remain standing.

The woman in black stood before me, a metal bowl in her hand. She set the bowl on the floor and looked quickly around the cell, as if she expected me to have discovered some means of escape.

"Please," I rasped, finding it hard to gather enough breath to speak. "I — had — a — bag."

Her eyes narrowed. "They say you claim to be innocent. If so, why did you have such a bag?"

Desperately I shook my head. "It — has things — all women —" I nearly choked on a mouthful of thick, bloody saliva.

Disbelief in her tone, she answered, "You will appear before a Magistrate in fifteen minutes. Do what you can to make yourself presentable."

With those words she opened the door wider and kicked my bag into the cell. The zipper was open and the contents spilled out. The comb slid toward the bucket and the soap rolled under the shelf, so I limped across the cell to retrieve them. Thankfully, the towel, toothbrush and underwear had not been removed.

I thought the guard might go away, but she watched as, with great difficulty, I rinsed off my body, then again, my headscarf and robe. With trembling hands I wet my hair, combed it from my face, and put on the scarf, tying it so that the dark bruise on my cheek was less visible. I feared the Magistrate would think I had angered the officers, and I could not afford to risk his wrath. I had no idea what might happen in the courtroom, but I knew from my many years as a slave that my life depended on what men with power saw when they turned their eyes on me.

Soon I was standing at the cell door, my face and body as clean as possible, headscarf and stained *djellaba* carefully arranged. The guard gestured for me to walk before her, and I staggered in agony from the cell, wondering whether I would ever return.

Slowed by the excruciating pain in my hip, it took what seemed a long, long time to walk through police headquarters. I managed to climb the stairs by pulling myself up by the railings, my shoulder throbbing, and once again I crossed the echoing hall. I followed the black robe into another part of the building and through a maze of identical corridors.

My guard knocked on a door, and soon a young woman in a flowered knee-length skirt, pale blouse, and glasses opened it. The guard stepped aside so I could enter, but remained just outside the door. I found myself in a small room filled with blinding, late morning sunlight. Delicate orchids in brass pots lined the windowsill, and colorful landscapes in matching frames hung on the opposite wall. There were two or three brocade-upholstered armchairs near the door. The young woman glanced at me and looked away quickly. Expressionless, she took a seat at her desk and I waited until she gestured that I should sit. Gratefully, I sank into a chair.

For some time there was no sound but the young woman typing. She ignored me, as if it were natural for her to sit beside a bruised, stinking woman. After some time a soft bell rang, and she spoke without looking up.

"You may go in now."

Heart thumping, I entered a spacious room. My swift glance took in dark-paneled shelves filled with leather-bound books. A wide wooden desk flanked bright windows and several chairs sat in a circle around a small, eight-sided table inlaid with mother-of-pearl. A rug in intricate patterns of beige and blue stretched across the floor. I stood still, sweating profusely, eyes lowered, and waited to be told what to do.

"You may be seated."

I was so shocked by the voice that I looked up. A woman in a navy jacket and skirt, dark hair swept into a thick knot at the back of her neck, stood at a cabinet, pouring coffee into a small cup.

To hide my surprise, I concentrated on crossing the room without limping and managed to sit without a sound.

The woman joined me at the little table, and picking up a folder of papers, took a sip of the coffee while reviewing the documents. A clock ticked in the corner. Beyond the windows I could hear the distant bleating of traffic. The smell of her coffee reminded me that it had been many hours since I'd eaten, and my stomach tightened, adding to the piercing pain in my hip and side. Despite it all, I noted the sound of her skirt shifting against her chair, the rose scent of her perfume, and the lazy swirling of the fan overhead.

Still reading, she asked, "Are you al-Magribhi Leila?" Her voice was deep, calm and not unpleasant.

"Yes, I am Leila," I answered, unsure whether to address her as "Magistrate."

"You seem very young," she observed and I looked up. Her face was handsome, with wide, *kohl*-shaded eyes and a fine mouth. She was wearing dark glasses that made her seem very wise, despite her young age. She did not react to my wet, stinking *djellaba* or swollen face.

"I don't know my birthdate," I answered, "but I left my home many years ago."

"Your file says you don't know the names of the people you worked for."

"I know their names," I admitted, "but I do not have the right to say them."

"Why not?"

For a moment I wavered. Did I dare admit my father had sold me to strangers? How would she react when I accused the judge — now the *Minister*! — of holding me as his slave?

"I — I was afraid."

"Of what?"

Again I looked at the floor.

"Why were you afraid?" she repeated quietly, but with an edge of impatience in her voice.

"I was merely a servant," I replied, "and at the time it seemed improper."

She weighed this for a moment, then returned to the file. "You are accused of theft, which is a very serious crime."

"I stole nothing," I answered, keeping my gaze fixed on the intricate rug.

"Yet you left your employer's home without his knowledge."

"It was time for me to seek a new life."

"And you found one here in Casablanca."

"I thank god for his blessings every day," I answered. She shifted in her seat and again sipped her coffee.

"Your accuser says you took jewelry of great value to his family."

"I know nothing of this," I said, straining through the pain to look into her face.

"So you left with nothing?"

"No — yes — I — I did take something," I said, still meeting her eyes. "I took clothes from my Young Mistress' closet."

"Clothes?"

"I had only the robes I wore when working. I took a clean blouse, pants, and sandals."

"So you did steal from her?"

"Only clothes. I took nothing more."

"You did not say this to the officers."

"I was afraid."

"How do I know you're telling the truth now?"

I struggled to find the words, then thought of Walid, who always spoke as simply and clearly as possible.

"When I came to Casablanca, I slept in a drainage pipe and begged for food on the streets. If I had stolen jewelry, I would not have been hungry or without a place to sleep."

"Perhaps the jewelry was lost or stolen."

"I took only the clothes."

Now she looked me over carefully, eyes taking in my damp clothing, still stained with blood and smelling dully of urine. Her gaze lingered on my scarred and swollen face.

Summoning more courage than I felt, I continued to keep my eyes raised.

"This is a difficult case," she observed. "You were arrested once before for theft."

"My Master was angry because I became lost in the souk during his son's wedding."

"You were stopped as you tried to leave the city with a man."

"I was afraid of being punished."

"Who was the man?"

"A stranger who agreed to help me."

"A stranger?" Her brows came together.

"He seemed to be kind," I whispered.

She sat back, a troubled expression on her face. "You're not making things easy for yourself, Madame. A very powerful person has made these accusations. He will want to see some action taken."

For a time she studied the papers. The minutes seemed to crawl by. Finally, she looked up.

"In this court it is not your accuser's responsibility to prove your guilt. The burden falls upon you to provide evidence of your innocence. Because of this, I do not have the authority to release you, especially in light of the seriousness of these accusations. On the other hand, the Minister has not provided us with descriptions of what was taken from his home, so the court is unable to determine exactly how you should be charged."

She paused. "I am aware it's been some time since the alleged theft occurred. This might have been settled much more easily had you not left Essaouira without making your former employer aware of your decision to go. That you came to Casablanca and began to use a new name strengthens his allegation that you're guilty. Do you understand?"

Feeling faint, I swayed forward, only managing to catch myself by grasping the edges of the chair. The Magistrate reached across the table and held my upper arm. "Are you sick?"

I nodded, fighting a sudden wave of nausea.

"What's wrong with you?"

If not for the bile rising in my throat, I might have remained silent. But I blurted the words: "I was beaten——"

"By whom?"

"The police offi——" Now a stream of clear, sour liquid rose up in my throat and I covered my mouth with my sleeve. She was on her feet and across the room in an instant, returning with a small trashcan.

I vomited a stream of bloody fluid into the trashcan and wiped my face with my hands. I heard her walk quickly to her desk, then return.

"Where are you injured?"

"My side," I answered weakly, "and my shoulder, my hip and ——"

"Your face," she said. There was another moment of silence. "How old are you?"

"Twenty-nine — perhaps — thirty."

"You are from the mountains?" she guessed.

I nodded, feeling another wave of nausea.

"Have you had formal education?"

I shook my head. My throat filled and I leaned forward, taking deep breaths.

"This is unacceptable," she muttered, turning away. "I will not be responsible for ——!"

She walked to her desk and picked up her phone, speaking in a low, urgent voice. When she returned to my side, I heard something different in her tone.

"Madame, I am sending you for immediate medical care. When the doctors release you, I expect you will be charged, taken into custody and held until a full investigation can be carried out. Hopefully you'll be able to satisfy the Minister that you are, indeed, telling the truth. I'm sorry, but there's nothing more I can do."

10. THE VULTURE

I had never set foot inside a hospital. I had been examined by a doctor only once in my life. Had I not been in so much pain I might have paid closer attention, but as soon as the black-robed guard walked me through the hospital's front doors, I became a broken doll in a toymaker's shop.

Limping heavily, I was led into a painfully bright room with rows of beds occupied by women. A woman in a white *djellaba* handed me a thin gown that didn't close in the back, and pointed to a bed beside a large blinking machine and a metal stand with plastic bags hung on its branches. She drew a curtain around the bed, but did not speak. I grew dizzy while undressing, and when my stinking clothes pooled on the floor I was unable to pick them up.

Still, when she returned I was leaning forward on the edge of the narrow mattress, struggling to breathe. She put my clothes into a plastic bag and vanished. Beneath the curtain I could see the hem of the guard's black robe.

A neatly bearded man in a white coat appeared. "I'm Doctor Mansouri," he announced briskly. "Please do your best to relax." Swiftly he shone a light into my eyes, ears and mouth. He listened to my heart through an instrument, as the doctor in the Women's Center had done years before, carefully examined the swelling on my face, then asked me to lie down.

I began to tremble as he pressed his hands through my gown along my chest and stomach. When I cried out he asked me to describe the pain. I had no words for it. For the first time he paused, focusing on my face. Becoming very still for a few moments, he then turned and vanished, only to come back with the woman in white, whom I now understood to be a nurse. He explained that he needed to examine me without my gown. The nurse carefully lifted the cloth.

I didn't want to see their expressions when my scars became visible, so I closed my eyes and clenched my teeth so tightly my jaw, too, began to ache.

The silence was long and weighted.

The doctor touched a thick ridge of skin along my collarbone. "Who did this to you?" he asked, his voice low.

"Another servant," I replied. My whole body had begun to shake.

"Why?"

"I — I displeased him," I rasped, snatching for breath.

The doctor's fingers probed the other scars on my chest. Carefully he lifted my right shoulder so he could examine my back. I screamed when my weight shifted onto my left hip. Gently he eased me back down on the bed.

After a moment he spoke very quietly. "When did you receive the wounds that caused those scars?"

"Seven years ago," I whispered.

"Did you receive medical care?"

I shook my head.

His hands moved expertly, massaging my ribcage. When he pressed on my hip I gasped in agony.

"This is very painful?"

I nodded.

"When did you receive these fresh bruises?"

"I believe — it was last night."

"You're not sure?"

"No."

"Were these new injuries caused by the same person?"

"No."

"Was it someone in your family?"

"No, it was —" I paused, hesitant to complete the sentence.

"Madame, I must know who perpetrated such violence against you."

Fear swallowed my words, but I glanced toward the black hem beneath the curtain. He turned, eyes following my gaze, and lowered his voice.

"Did someone strike your head?"

"I fell — against the wall."

"Did you pass out?"

"I'm not sure."

"Does your head hurt now?"

I nodded.

"Let me know where it hurts most," he said as he cradled my head in one hand and ran his fingers skillfully along my skull. I cried out again when he touched my temple.

"Follow my finger with your eyes," he said, staring into my face. "When was the last time you had food?"

"I — I don't know."

"Have you been nauseated?"

I nodded, feeling hot tears explode from my eyes, pour down my cheeks and dampen the sheets. He blotted my cheeks with a handkerchief, then shone a tiny light into my eyes.

Suddenly my exhaustion drowned out the pain and I felt myself drift. The air surrounding the bed shimmered, and the sound of my breath in my ears was louder than the noise beyond the curtain. The doctor continued his examination, but now nothing hurt and I didn't care that no one knew where I was.

I could see him speaking words I couldn't understand. The curtain swished open, then closed. I felt his hand as he lifted my filthy, bloodstained fingers.

"Are you married, Madame?" he asked in a slow, deliberate voice.

I managed another nod, though I realized with a swelling sadness that someone had taken my wedding ring.

"Will you tell me your husband's name?"

"Al-Magribhi Walid."

"Has your husband ever hit you?"

"No!" My answer was louder than I intended, and he made a calming sound.

"That's fine, Madame. We're going to need to conduct x-rays of your ribs and hip. But before we do, I need to ask you just a few more questions. When did you last have your monthly blood?"

I fought for clarity from my wheeling thoughts and managed to open my eyes. The doctor wrote something on a clipboard, his face expressionless.

"I — I don't know. What day is it?"

"Thursday, January 31st," he answered.

I tried to remember when I'd last bled, but that, too, was impossible.

"That's alright," he said as he felt the skin around my ankles. "Are your legs often swollen like this?"

Once again, I couldn't answer.

"Madame, would you allow me to examine the rest of your body? This may be difficult for you. Please don't be alarmed."

If I hadn't been in such pain I might have protested as he pressed my breasts and belly, then put on plastic gloves and probed between my legs. By now I wept openly, hands covering my eyes.

The nurse returned, pushing a bed on wheels.

"We won't need that after all," he said to her, stepping away and pulling the curtain closed. His voice blended into the sea of sound, light and pain.

When he returned, he leaned close to me.

"Madame, we're not going to x-ray you. Instead, we have a new machine we can use to look at your body. It takes longer than the x-ray, but it's almost as effective. This will not cause you any discomfort.

"Very soon I will give you something to help with the pain. I will also ask for some lentil soup for you. It may not be very good — our hospital kitchen is not known for its cuisine, but until we're sure you haven't sustained a head injury, we must be careful not to give you something that could cause you to choke. Do you understand?"

I nodded.

He moved closer to me. "Will you please tell me your name?"

"Al-Magribhi Leila," I whispered.

"May I call you Leila?" he asked, his voice gentle. Again I nodded.

"Please look at me, Leila."

Reluctantly, I complied. I found his dark eyes only inches from mine.

"I've been a doctor for some years, but I confess I've never before had a patient accompanied by a vulture. What has a little sparrow like you done to be hunted by a bird of prey?" His eyes flitted toward the black robe of my guard, still visible beneath the curtain.

"Don't be afraid, Leila. I don't know who hurt you in the past, but it's clear to me that you are very, very strong. Not many people could have survived what you've gone through."

He leaned back, considered me, then gently drew his fingers along my scarred face, wiping my tears away.

The curtain opened and a metal box with what resembled a small television screen was wheeled up to the bed.

"Now," he said as he stood. "Please do your best to relax. The next few minutes are very, very important. I promise no one will hurt you. You're safe, here."

There are those who understand that peace is always close, should we choose to seek it. Selina and Walid are among them. That's why it was fitting that when I awakened from a sleep so deep it felt like death, it was the nearly identical faces of mother and son that greeted me.

Selina was perched on the edge of the bed, her tiny body stretched almost as far as she could reach, so she could hold me, and Walid stood behind her, one hand on my good shoulder, the other touching the place on my forehead he had just kissed. The curtain had been drawn around us, protecting us from the curiosity of the other patients and my guard, whose black robes hovered like a shadow.

"Leila," Selina whispered, "we're here. The young doctor called us."

Struggling against a desire to drift off, I fought to form a few hoarse words: "I'm so sorry, Mother —"

Selina moved her fingers to my lips. "There is no reason to apologize!"

"Walid —" I whispered, "they took my ring —"

He kissed me again. "I'll get you another ring, Leila. The doctor says you must rest and think of nothing until you're better."

I stirred, feeling weighed down, as if something heavy had been placed on my chest. I wore another thin gown covered only by a sheet, but my body was so warm the mattress beneath me was wet.

Trying to raise my head, I discovered it was wrapped in bandages. My shoulder, too, was bound tightly, with my right arm pinned across my chest. Thin tubes inserted into the inside of my arm at the wrist were held in place with strips of tape. Most uncomfortable, however, was my left leg, which was encased in a cast extending from my waist to my knee.

"Please listen," Walid said, his tone so controlled that only someone who knew him well would hear his rage. "Your hip is fractured, several ribs are broken and your shoulder was dislocated. You also have a minor concussion, and —" his voice tripped over the words, "and your cheekbone was broken again."

Walid's eyes were very dark and his thin cheeks seemed to have grown even more hollow. Most of all, I could see that his body was as rigid as stone.

Selina wiped her tears with the butt of her hand. "This was done to you by the police?"

"Yes, but my hip was hurt before, when —"

"— Those animals beat you!" She stroked my face. "Leila, we won't let them take you from us. Do you understand? You're never going back to that place!"

"Mother's right," Walid added. "We will find a way to protect you."

A machine beeped wildly, and Walid pulled the curtain open and vanished. Within seconds, he returned with a nurse, who lifted my free hand, examined a clamp on my finger and adjusted a dial on the monitor. When the beeping quieted, she told Selina and Walid they could stay only a few moments longer.

I gestured to Selina and she leaned close. "How long have I been here?"

"Two days. They took you from the tearoom five days ago."

"I can't remember —"

"Good. It's better if you don't."

"How long must I stay here?"

"Until you're well again."

"But the tearoom —"

"Everything will be fine. Aliah's daughter will help out after school and Shada has agreed to work more."

I looked from her face to Walid's. His forced smile had faded and a new emotion filled his eyes.

Selina kissed me and stood. "We'll bring food for you tomorrow. For now, you must rest and think of nothing. Promise me you won't worry, beloved daughter!"

Walid turned to his mother. "May I speak to Leila alone?"

He pulled a chair next to the bed and leaned close to me. Carefully he took my hand.

"I will never forgive myself for letting this happen."

"This was not your fault, Walid."

His voice tightened. "You must do what the doctor tells you. He will do his best, but it will take time to heal."

He stopped speaking, but the look in his eyes cleared my thoughts.

"I'm not going to die, Walid."

He swallowed.

"*I will not leave you*," I said.

He lowered his head so I wouldn't see his tears, then held my hands until the nurse insisted he go.

I am made of pain.

My world is a mattress, my nation a rectangle bordered by metal. I smell of sweat, blood and the ointments used to soothe the cast's chafing. Food has no taste and sound is senseless without sight. I can see no further than the curtain that swallows my bed.

I weep at night.

I cannot stop.

I press the sheet into my mouth so no one can hear.

Sometimes I no longer wish to breathe.

The vulture has not gone away. She keeps watch throughout the night and day.

She will not allow me another chance at freedom.

Before dawn each day Walid and Selina arrive with drinks of fresh yogurt and mashed fruits. They return in the evenings with *homous*, lentil soup and finely chopped chicken breasts. Selina feeds me spoonfuls of silken rice pudding and raisins, complaining all the while that I'm not eating enough. Hania's visits in the early afternoon are welcome by the hospital staff, who enjoy the sweet rolls and *griouches* she brings.

Each and every day their bags are searched by the vulture, who pretends my family might have weapons. And each day, the woman in black takes a portion of the food. This enrages Selina, but Walid calms his mother, warning that the vulture could cause me harm. Mouth tight with rage, Selina wipes my arms, neck and forehead with a cool, damp cloth, while murmuring a song about a warrior who strikes his enemies dead like a flash of lightening in a mountain valley.

Hania spends her afternoon visits chattering about a bright and glittering world beyond the curtain: beautiful actresses finding their husbands cheating with their best friends. Members of the royal family blackmailed by their butlers. Wild parties of government officials in London and Rome. So far-fetched are her tales that I awake later and wonder if I've imagined them.

Walid brings books of poetry and folktales, including the *Arabian Nights,* and reads them to me. Many years ago my Young Master taught me to read the first chapter of the *Arabian Nights*, and though I'd sometimes wondered what became of the beautiful, brave Scheherazade, my memories of those afternoons always end with images of the nights Young Master waited in the darkness to rape me.

Walid doesn't know this, and I have neither the heart nor strength to tell him. In truth, I can barely understand his words through my ever-flowing river of pain, but the quiet rhythm of his voice often lulls me to sleep. I awaken to a nurse checking my blood pressure, and find him sitting beside me, haunted eyes anchored to mine, his voice etching a gentle, near-whispered song.

Though the pain never lessened, after five days Dr. Mansouri determined I had made enough progress to be moved from the nurses' station to the far end of the ward, where I'd have more privacy.

The vulture protested when the nurses unhooked the machines next to my bed. When she challenged him, the doctor told her she had no authority over his wing of the hospital, and if she didn't remain at the nurses' station he would have her removed. I was shocked by his words, and even more surprised by her sudden silence. Perhaps, I supposed, *all* women were subject to a man's authority, even when they wore the black robes of power.

The curtain that had contained my pain was swept aside, and I was wheeled into a long, bright hall of two-dozen beds, all occupied by women who watched as the nurses pushed me to a far corner beside a window.

During my slow, strange journey the other patients stared with open curiosity. Several had casts on their arms and legs, though at least one was bandaged as if badly beaten or burned.

Their few possessions were placed on small bedside tables. They fanned themselves against the heat, expressions dull. A television, bolted to the wall in the center of the room, came into view. Four rusty fans turned in lopsided rotations on the ceiling, high overhead.

Once in my corner, another curtain was pulled around my bed. But now I had a window, and though the lower panes were frosted, the upper panes afforded me a wide-open view of the sky, where a pair of white gulls wheeled gloriously on the breeze before soaring seaward.

Dr. Mansouri removed the bandages from my ribs as the nurse stood by with the viewing machine.

"Now Leila, do you remember the day you were first brought to the hospital? We used this machine, which is called a sonogram, to check for broken bones. Do you understand?"

I nodded; it still hurt to speak. The nurse turned on the machine, which made a low humming noise, and the doctor squirted clear jelly on my body and carefully rubbed a wand back and forth over my skin. An oval image appeared on the small television. For a few moments there was nothing in the sea of gray, then suddenly I could make out strange shapes and shadows that seemed to shift and pulse. The machine throbbed, like the beating of my heart. Without meaning to, I closed my fists tighter around the railings of the bed.

He moved on to my shoulder. Then he turned his attention to my hip. This took time, for my body had to be shifted on the bed so he could find a space for his wand. The nurse assisted him in moving me, and the agony caused by the weight of the cast made me shriek, despite my best effort to remain silent.

When I was once again on my back, soaked through with sweat and gasping for breath, Dr. Mansouri sent the nurse for ice water and a fresh gown. He turned off the machine and sat beside me for some time, wiping my tears and speaking reassuringly.

"Don't cry, Madame. I know you're exhausted and afraid, but trust me: you are going to survive this. All will come right in the end."

After some time the pain lessened to a dull roar, and I was able to focus on the folds of the curtain, the blue sky beyond the window, and finally, the bearded man still waiting patiently beside me.

"Leila," the doctor said, "I will try to explain everything that's happened in the past few days, and what should happen in the near future.

"I suspect your fall at the police station fractured your hip on the site of an older injury, perhaps something that happened years ago and never properly healed. Our surgeon inserted a pin that will strengthen the bones so you can walk normally again."

He leaned toward me, speaking very clearly. "The surgeon also reset your shoulder and removed two small slivers of bone from your thigh. He rebuilt the bridge of your nose with one so you'll breathe better, and placed the other in your broken cheek. You will always have a scar, but it will be far less visible than before your surgery."

He smiled reassuringly.

"You don't have to worry. The surgeon is a close friend of mine from university who specializes in such operations. He has some years of experience and was more than pleased to take on this challenge."

He leaned closer. "Just so you know, I'm married to his favorite sister, and he'd never do anything to make her unhappy."

To my surprise, I laughed. The sound was high and rough — a kind of scratching across the surface of my throat, for anything that came from inside of me was torture.

"I intend to remove the bandages from your face tomorrow. If your sonograms continue to improve, you'll be out of the cast in five to six weeks. Then, as soon as you're walking, you'll invite me to lunch at your family's famous tearoom. It must be a wonderful place. The nurses can't stop talking about the delicious bread and pastries."

He glanced over his shoulder toward the end of the ward, where I knew the black robe watched.

"I've never before had a patient whom I've been ordered to keep behind a curtain, with her own personal guard. Many people in the hospital believe you must be a famous celebrity or a member of the royal family. But I know the truth. You, Leila, are far closer to an angel."

11. SLAVE

Like Dr. Mansouri, the surgeon, Dr. Bennouna, wore a short, neatly trimmed beard and spoke with a confidence that belied his young age.

He removed the bandages from my face and the two doctors stood beside the bed, observing me critically. Dr. Mansouri smiled at his brother-in-law and patted him gently on the back. A nurse produced a mirror, but I motioned for her to take it away.

"Madame?" the surgeon began, but Dr. Mansouri touched his arm. "She'll look when she's ready."

Once alone, I reached up to touch my nose, eye socket and cheek. I discovered a slick, almost silken patch of skin and a milder indentation where once there'd been a thickened ridge of scar. The bridge of my nose was swollen, but no longer crushed. I could breathe without wheezing.

Hania paused at the curtain when she came to visit that afternoon. Her expression melted into a smile, and Selina clasped her hands together. "God be praised," she said softly.

"Please stop," I said, when Hania began describing my face.

"But Leila —"

"I will judge for myself when this is finally over."

It was Walid, however, whose eyes captured my deeply confused emotions.

"Well?" I asked, searching his face.

"Many will find you lovelier," he answered, "but my wish is simple: I hope your face will no longer exile you from the world."

Though I told no one, the woman in black slipped inside the curtain and appeared beside my bed every night, when the ward was quiet and the nurses had withdrawn from their station to some deeper part of the hospital.

I don't know why she waited until the darkest hours to walk the length of the quiet ward and step inside my curtain. Perhaps she first came to defy the doctor's authority, or to exert her own sense of power. Perhaps it was simply to satisfy her curiosity about the woman hidden on the orders of a man of wealth and privilege beyond her imagining.

One night I opened my eyes when I heard the curtain move, and watched the vulture draw close in the square of moonlight. Swallowed by her robes, the little I could see of the woman's face was weathered; her heavy brows met above dark eyes and a fading village tattoo slashed her forehead. When she moved toward me I smelled sweat and unwashed flesh, and when she spoke her breath was foul.

"So, tonight you do not pretend," she said in the poetic language of my people. I was surprised, and saddened, to learn that she, too, was from the mountains, yet it also made me bold.

"What do you seek, Mother, that can only be found in the darkness?"

"All who snore do not sleep," she answered. "The day has eyes, so the night must have ears."

"An egg cannot break a rock. Can't you see that I am hurt?"

"I believe every part of you is false."

"Then, you believe this to be untrue?" Carefully I pulled the thin sheet from my cast and heavily bandaged shoulder.

She stared without speaking.

"Craft may have its clothes, but the truth is naked," I said. "I cannot flee. I can do nothing to protect myself. Have you come to harm me?"

To my surprise, she bent closer. I turned my head at her unwashed smell.

"The fish on the hook is quick to think," she declared. "You are not the first to claim injury to avoid justice."

"Mother, every dawn, noon and night I pray that justice finds me. No matter what you've been told, I've harmed no person on earth."

"So say all deceivers."

"Turn on the light. Look into my eyes. Do you find deceit?"

Oddly, she did stare into my face. For a brief instant, though I don't know what she saw in my eyes, I could read the fear in hers.

She drew back as if stung. Her brows came together and I thought she might strike me.

"The greatest passion is compassion," I whispered, quickly closing my eyes. "I want nothing more than to go home to those I love and who love me."

"Do you think yourself more worthy of love than the rest of us? Do you think I wish to spend my days in this place full of sickness, keeping watch over you?"

"You can walk, and I cannot. You may smell the sea breeze, and I cannot. Your word is trusted, and mine is not. Please, Mother: only the person carrying the load knows the weight of the stones."

She stood in silence for what seemed a long time. The air between us loosened, as if the knots holding the ends of a rope had slipped.

"What is your name?" I whispered.

"That is not for you to know."

"In my village it was often said that if a man falls, all will tread on him. Was this not also said in yours?"

She paused, then drew closer. "Tala. They called me Tala."

"What do you seek?"

"I seek the truth about Essaouira."

"To welcome truth, you must first banish disbelief."

"I will believe when the truth is told."

"Then my answer is simple: I served until I could serve no more."

Beyond the curtain someone coughed. The machine beside the bed clicked out a rhythm. I shifted to relieve the weight of the cast.

"How did you come to be there?" she asked, her voice a dry rustle in the darkness.

"I was a child who could not speak for herself."

"You had no father?"

"No, though he lived in our home and was wed to my mother."

"You give fault to him for your life?"

"My life was traded for his debts."

"Yet you paid his debts poorly."

"I gave up my flesh, my freedom and my purity. Little was left to be taken."

"You stole from your Master."

"Believe what you see, and lay aside what you have heard."

"You are not to be believed."

"It is worse to be wounded by words than a sword, Mother. Some would say that if the judge is against me, I should withdraw my complaint. But even if I speak only to silence, I still must speak."

There was another long pause as she weighed her response.

"You thought they would forget you."

"I know well the hawk forever seeks the sparrow."

"You have crafted your words to hide your lies."

"The story is only half told when one side tells it."

"Your Master will not release you," she said curtly.

"Hope must be the last thing to die," I replied.

"Do not bother to hope," she retorted, moving back to the curtain." He will not set you free. Of this I am sure. He has never freed me."

I should have reasoned that I was neither the first, nor the last, to serve in the house above the sea.

Had Tala been the servant of my Master's mother, years before my time?

Had she perhaps cared for Young Master during his childhood?

All the following day I pondered it, yet I said nothing to Selina or Walid. Though I understood the vulture could easily harm me, I sensed there was something she wanted — and I was safe until she satisfied her need.

Perceptive as always, Walid noticed my distraction during their morning visit. After Selina talked about the tearoom, he asked about my pain, my appetite, my reading, and listened more to the sound of my voice than to my answers.

Before they left, Selina pressed a handful of *dinars* into my palm. "Your portion of the money for the past few weeks," she said as I shook my head. "Ask the nurse for ice cream or a cool drink if we're not here to buy them for you."

"Mother —"

"I'll hide it here," she insisted, sliding the notes into an empty space beneath the drawer of the bedside table. "Don't argue. Everyone wants you to have it."

Walid smiled as his mother disappeared behind the curtain. "We miss you," he explained. "It helps us to pretend you're still there." Kissing my forehead, a question lingered in his eyes. "Leila, is anything —"

"I'm fine, Walid," I said firmly.

He wavered. Perhaps fearing he'd add to my distress, he decided against finishing his question. "I'll be back after work this evening," he promised.

Late that night Tala returned and, black robe heavy with odor, settled beside me.

"Now you understand," she said, her words muffled by the cloth drawn around her face.

"They never spoke of you or any others."

"Why do you think there were others?"

"The family is as old as the house itself."

"I am an old woman."

"Not old enough."

"You know nothing about me."

"And you," I whispered, "know nothing of me."

Her silence was less threatening than the night before. Still, I knew that one should befriend a dog without laying down one's stick.

"What do you seek?" I asked again. Her odor lingered like a veil between us.

"The truth," she again answered. "They say that man who visits is your husband, but if he knew about your past, he would not want you."

"Many are the roads that lead to the heart."

"Not for whores and thieves."

"I am neither, despite what they told you."

"Why would they lie?"

"Because they can."

Her long silence ended in a murmur. "I cannot trust what is said in shadow."

"Then we will sit in shadow but speak in light."

"You will tell me," she said, "what it was like for you in Essaouira."

I lay very still, thinking. She had lived there before me. She had likely known the old woman and Hassan. What could I tell her she didn't already know?

Then Selina's voice entered my mind: *the bear knows many songs, all of them about honey.*

"Tala," I said thoughtfully, "do you remember the way the water sings in the fountain in the courtyard?"

"Yes."

"And how the house breathes with the changing tides?"

"Surely."

"You know which passage to take when you make your way from the *souk*—"

"I asked what it was like for *you*," she repeated testily.

"You ask me to speak of how steep the stairs were beneath the weight of the tray? To describe the bell late at
night, when my Old Mistress —"

"Do not mock me, thief!" she spat. "You will tell me
what no one else knows."

"Some things are better left unspoken."

"You will share them with me."

"I'm afraid," I confessed in a whisper. "Essaouira
haunts me, Mother, and to speak of it gives it life."

A rattle I knew was laughter escaped from her robes.
"Of course you are afraid," she answered, "but you will
tell me the truth because I want to know, and —" her voice
flattened — "no one *else* will ever really understand."

She was right.

Though I loved, and was loved by Walid, Hania and
Selina, there were parts of me they could never truly know.
How many times since I arrived on their doorstep had they
argued against the logic of my fear? How many nights had
they stood by, helpless, as I struggled against my past? What
were the limits of love to heal, to protect, and to truly bear
the weighted silence of memory?

This ragged woman sitting beside me — the agent of
my Master — was the vision of what I was destined to become, had I not fled Essaouira.

Turning my face toward her, I breathed in the stench of
her slavery.

"Tala," I murmured, "listen and I will turn your ears
into eyes."

With simple words I unspooled the thread of my life,
from the moment I arrived in Essaouira, until my escape
to Casablanca. Though I don't know how it happened, I
found I could speak about pain I had buried deeper than
memory. My time in the brothel, the kindness of Bahia;

the years of darkness in the house above the sea — it all poured forth, as she listened in silence. Tears coursed from my eyes, but I did not sob. I did not tremble. And I did not lie.

As I finished, exhausted, dawn crept toward the windowpane.

"Your husband and his mother will be here soon," she observed as she stood, clutching her hood close to her face. "It is strange they seem to care so much about you. Don't they understand you've earned your punishment?"

"I have done nothing wrong," I said, stung by her words.

"You have shown no respect for your Master, the Minister," she replied, slipping behind the curtain.

12. The Mirror

D r. Mansouri seemed genuinely happy when he snapped off the sonogram and asked the nurse to wheel it away. Once we were alone, he put my chart on the floor and moved his chair a hairbreadth from the bed.

"You're improving very quickly, Madame. Your hip has healed beautifully over the past six weeks, and I think the cast should come off soon. You've gained weight, too. I was very concerned about how thin you were when you first came in."

He gave me a measuring look.

"Now Leila, please listen carefully. I've hesitated to say anything because of the seriousness of your injuries, but it's becoming critical that you know."

I search his eyes. "Is something wrong?"

"On the contrary." He reached for my hands. You, Madame al-Magribhi, are with child."

I heard a strange rushing sound, like a high wind through the crack of a window being closed. Though I had, indeed, missed my monthly blood, I had often stopped bleeding for months when I lived in Essaouira.

He smiled at my astonishment.

"I discovered your pregnancy when you arrived at the hospital in early February. I made a decision, based on your condition, to tell you and your husband only when I was sure the baby survived. You were so badly hurt, I honestly believed you would lose the child, and I feared that such a tragedy would delay your recovery.

"It's a true miracle you didn't miscarry when you were beaten by that policeman. In many cases, such a shock might indeed trigger a miscarriage. I called my brother-in-law to discuss what he could do. He took special care during the surgery and through it all, your baby has thrived. The sonogram suggests you're well into your fourth month."

"Fourth month?" I repeated vaguely.

"I apologize to you, Leila. I know you've suffered these many weeks, but I withheld the strongest pain medication because it might have harmed your child. I believed that given the choice, you'd have urged me to work for the safety of the baby."

"I — I didn't think I was able to — "

"It's often difficult for a woman to conceive when she is very thin, malnourished, or under extreme duress. I don't know what happened in your past, but judging from your scars, I can well imagine that the conditions you experienced might have interfered with normal ovulation.

"What I mean," he explained to my confused expression, "is that sometimes it takes months, or even years, for the body to recover from such stress."

"Are you sure the baby will live?"

"Normally, after the first three months we worry less about miscarriage. Of course, your injuries make this a special case."

"Does Walid know?"

"Not yet. I thought you should have the pleasure of telling him."

Now, despite my joy, I closed my eyes.

"Is something the matter?"

"Walid was married once before. His wife died in childbirth, and he lost his son a few days later. If our child survives, he'll be the happiest man on earth. But if I lose this baby —" I paused. "Please, don't tell Walid until we're sure."

"Leila, I —"

"*Please.*"

The doctor looked at me curiously. "You've been through so much, yet you worry more about others than about yourself. Alright, Leila. I'll say nothing to your husband, or the other members of your family, until you give me permission to do so."

I reached for his arm as he began to rise. "Doctor Mansouri, I must ask you one more thing."

"Yes, Leila?"

"Do you know what I've been accused of?"

"I've heard rumors, but I can't concern myself with police affairs."

"If they arrest me, what will happen to my child?"

"It all depends on whether you're held in a prison," he said guardedly. "A healthy woman can give birth almost anywhere. But if you are not completely healed, it would be dangerous for you to give birth outside a hospital."

"Doctor," I said, holding his arm more tightly, "my mother always said that pregnancy, like riding on a camel, can never be hidden. That woman — the vulture — must not know."

"My mother often said that dogs may bark," he responded, "but the caravan passes on. No matter what you've been accused of, your child has the right to be protected. We'll keep your pregnancy private as long as possible. For now, I want you to put all your energy into resting, eating well and getting out of this bed."

He smiled. "If all goes well, you'll not only give birth next September, but you'll be able to push the baby carriage up the steepest hill in Casablanca."

Briskly he stood and moved toward the curtain. "By the way, I tasted some of your mother-in-law's lentil soup.

It was uncommonly delicious. Do they serve it in your famous tearoom, along with those wonderful pastries?"

"Yes, every day."

"Then I must make a note to start taking my lunches there!"

"Doctor—"

He looked back, the tails of his white coat striking the curtain.

"I haven't seen my face since the surgery."

For a moment I expected another of his jokes, but instead he returned to his seat beside the bed.

"Why not?"

"I was afraid to see a slave."

"A slave?"

"I mean — a woman without hope."

"The hardest battles are against the self," he said quietly. "I've never had a patient like you."

Reaching into the drawer of the bedside table, he removed the mirror and pressed it against his chest.

"You will find, when you see yourself, that my brother-in-law was able to restore the shape of your nose and broken cheek. The scar is much less prominent, but you will carry its mark forever."

He paused. "Though my brother-in-law has once again proven he deserves his reputation, I think your beauty has caused you great pain. I hope your face will be a source of happiness in the years to come."

He turned the mirror toward me. "Are you ready to meet yourself?"

"Yes," I answered. "I need to learn the face my child will know as its mother."

❖ ❖ ❖

I studied Walid when he visited that evening. Though still outwardly calm, anger and frustration lived close to the surface of his gaze. Unlike Hania, who remained stubbornly cheerful, his inability to protect me had made him bitter. Though learning of the baby would bring him joy, I sensed the news would also seem yet another burden, so pushing aside my guilt at keeping the child a secret, I focused on his words.

"I'm working with a lawyer to find a way to remove that woman," he said, inclining his head toward the end of the ward. "I've tried to speak with hospital officials, but no one will see me or return my calls."

Touching his arm, I found his body tense beneath my fingers.

"The hospital," he continued, "has strict rules about visitors, yet they'll permit her to sleep in the hall and eat our food until the day she decides to have you arrested again."

"They fear the Minister's reprisals."

"But why does she do it? She has no quarrel with you."

"She knows no other way to live."

"What do you mean?"

"When I was a slave, I thought like a slave. It took me years to learn how to be free."

"What do you know of her?" he asked, staring at me.

I drew in a breath. "She comes to me at night, Walid. I've spoken with her several times."

"Are you insane?" he said sharply. "If you befriend a vulture, you'll lose your eyes!"

I started, surprised at his anger.

Calming himself, he touched the side of my face, so I'd have to meet his eyes.

"I'm begging you to be wise, Leila. Tell her nothing about yourself, or your life. They'll use your words against you."

I nodded, knowing he was right. Learning my deepest secrets had done nothing to lessen Tala's hostility toward me.

Walid reached over to wipe away the tears that suddenly flooded my eyes.

"I'm sorry, my love. I didn't mean to be unkind."

"I'm not hurt," I replied, honestly. "I'm tired. Most of my life I've been afraid to walk in the sunlight, speak my thoughts aloud, or to look in people's eyes. I spent over six years in hiding, yet it protected me from nothing. Long before they found me I was held captive by my fear. No matter what happens when I leave this bed, I can no longer live that way."

His face brightened in surprise. As if by instinct, he placed a hand on my stomach. I reached down and brought his fingers to my lips.

"We're going to survive this, Walid. I don't know how, but we're going to find a way to be free."

I thought deeply all the following day. While listening to Hania's chatter about an actress who adopted five children, I pondered what I must do to gain some power over my life. By the time Tala slipped inside the curtain, settling beside me in the darkness, I had decided I would use our conversations as one must risk a field of thorns before picking the perfect rose.

"You have listened to my truth," I began softly, "yet still you find fault with me."

"We must live the life we are given," she answered.

"What of your life, Tala?"

"Into a closed mouth no fly may enter."

"A closed mouth soon starves. Speak to me, Mother, and let me rest a while from my pain."

"You have earned your pain, thief."

"If I am a thief, why are you by my side? My words would be no different if I told you my tale a thousand and one times."

Tala shifted inside her black robes and I thought I heard her laugh. "Only a brave bird makes its nest in a cat's ear. What can I tell *you* that you don't already know about Essaouira?"

"Tell me," I answered quietly, "why those with so much power were always so cruel."

A reflective silence followed. In the ward beyond the curtain someone murmured in her sleep.

The black robes rustled. "It was his mother," she said in a low voice, "who destroyed them."

The air was suddenly taut with the weight of confession. "Who was destroyed?"

"She destroyed them all, but the judge's wife was first." In the darkness I could make out the dull gleam of Tala's eyes, staring into space, her thoughts far away.

"The judge's wife?" I murmured. The memory of a conversation held many years before, shortly after my arrival in the judge's house, flooded my mind. I was speaking with Rabah, a woman who helped with the cooking.

"What of my Master's wife?"

"She died in childbirth. The boy never knew her."

"And the old Mistress is the Master's mother?"

"Yes, the old woman is his mother. Who knows? Perhaps he might have found another wife if his mother had been less of a burden. Despite his wealth and social position, no other woman has ever been acceptable to her."

"Who cared for the old woman before I came?"

"There have been others — mostly widows who needed the work and were willing to spend the day sitting with her. You are the first to be so — young."

"I came to this house pure, and I remain so," I responded proudly...

Now Tala stirred.

"The judge's wife was beautiful, joyful and young, and at first he loved her. Though the marriage was quickly made, all saw that they were happy."

"And then?"

"The old woman, the Master's mother, became jealous. She hated her son's wife — hated that he found no fault in her, that there was laughter in their rooms in the dark. After she bore the judge a son, the old woman saw her as a rival."

"I don't understand. Didn't the judge's wife die in childbirth?"

"Of course not! With Hassan's help they held her there, in the other part of the house, and would not let her leave."

"But how?"

"The old woman told her son his wife was a whore, who met with other men while he was in the courts. She convinced him his wife could not be trusted. She said his wife was unworthy of their name, and they had to protect the boy from her."

"And the judge agreed to this?"

"He could not risk his family's reputation, so he chose to believe his mother."

"And his son?"

"He was only a small child, and he missed his mother very much. Whenever he cried, his grandmother struck him. Soon he learned to make no sound."

Now I glanced toward the figure in the darkness.

"You took care of my Master's mother, didn't you? You spent your days in her room. You washed her, prepared her food and carried it up those stairs —"

"It was not so difficult in my day," the voice replied. "She still had her vision and could walk a little. Still, she knew she was going blind, and wanted her grandson beside her night and day. He slept in the room outside her bedchamber, and when he asked about his mother, she said horrible things — things no child should hear. He learned to hate his mother, too, in time."

"And they kept her there, in the house?"

"Only Hassan was permitted to see her."

"Why didn't the Master divorce her?"

A bitter, choking laugh emerged. "It was the money, of course."

"I don't understand."

"The marriage gave his name to her family, and her wealth to his."

"But I thought —"

"Yes, they pretend to be rich, but when I lived there much of the house was closed, and they never had servants enough to run it."

"Did her family not try to protect her?"

"Did your family try to protect you?"

My thoughts spun. Though I knew years ago my life was forfeit for my father's debts, could a family of means reason the same way?

"What happened to her?" I asked.

"She hanged herself one night. She had not been seen for so long, most believed she died during the birth of the child."

"And now," I whispered, "how do they live?"

Tala laughed again.

"A good marriage was made for the judge's son — good enough to assure him a position as a diplomat, and the judge the post of Minister."

"Is her family so powerful?"

"Their power is their wealth, as wealth is often the key to power."

"But is it not the groom's father who must offer payment for the bride?"

"The Senhaji name is one of the oldest in Essaouira. For her father, it was payment, enough."

My heart nearly bursting, I stared in the direction of her voice.

"Does Young Master treat his wife the way his father treated his mother?"

"Your Young Master needs a wife who will give up her life for his success. In this, I think she was well chosen."

"Then she's happy with Young Master?"

"Like any loyal wife, she has accepted the life she's been given. But you would know better than I if are they happy," Tala added. "Were you not there when they married?"

"Yes."

"Then I make you the judge: was your Young Master true to his bride, or did he seek pleasure with others?" Her eyes glittered maliciously.

"Tala —" I asked cautiously, "why were you no longer in Essaouira when I arrived?"

A long silence followed; she began to rock very faintly from side to side.

"I came as one," she said, "but left as two."

I came to this house pure, and I remain so.

"You had no husband —"

"I had no husband by day, but I was sometimes married at night."

I came to this house pure, and I remain so.

"You bore a child while living in that house?"

"Mountain girls know many things," she answered, "but little about men with power."

"The judge sent you away with his child?"

"His mother would not allow an unmarried girl who had given birth to remain in the house."

"But the child was her blood!"

"My boy was his bastard, not his blood."

"Your son does not bear the name of his father?"

"A child made in darkness has no father."

"Then why do your Master's bidding, now?"

"My child and I were never hungry, and when he became a man, he received a commission in the army."

"Yet still you work for the Master against me?"

"Fool!" she spat. "You have a husband, and I have none. You have work that feeds you, and I do not. I cannot read or write, or return to my own home at night. Why should I beg on the streets? The Minister protects me, and keeps me safe. My service assures the future of my son."

"Then," I said, "you will never be free."

Angrily, she rose. "How would your idea of freedom serve me?"

13. THE HOUR

The music of patients' voices ceased abruptly, as it did whenever someone new entered the ward, and I glanced up from my wheelchair expectantly. The cast had been removed, and now I sat with my leg propped up, Aisha's book of poetry in my lap. Between the powerful, stirring poems that seemed to explode in my mind, my thoughts returned stubbornly to the history revealed to me by Tala.

Walid appeared; kissing my forehead, he announced in a falsely bright voice that my cousins Hamid and Tadiah had traveled all the way from Marrakech to visit me.

Though I had never met such cousins, I quickly smoothed my hair, which had grown long enough to braid into a loose plait, and drew my *kaftan* tight around my shoulders.

A slender man in a fine white burnoose stepped around the curtain, leaned forward and kissed both my cheeks, saying, "Leila, we're all so glad to hear you're better."

Behind him stood the figure, in a traditional dark headscarf and *djellaba*, of Fatima, though Aisha was nowhere to be seen.

"Leila," Fatima murmured as she, too, bent to kiss me, "I'm so sorry it's taken us so long to visit."

"We're very lucky today," Walid remarked sarcastically. "Despite all expectations, your guard, for some reason, seemed to be sleeping when we passed her in the hall."

The stranger, a man with short, curly hair and a well-groomed moustache, smelled of Egyptian sandalwood mixed with bergamot. He might have been a Tunisian, but for the dark honey tone of his eyes. For reasons I couldn't grasp, his face took me back to the *souk* of Essaouira.

Khalil's gaze lingered on the troubled traces of my scar. He shifted uneasily, and peered at his hands.

Fatima, however, pulled off her headscarf and shook her hair loose. "I bring you greetings from Aisha. She wanted to join us, but the hospital's rules are so strict, we knew we'd be lucky if Khalil and I made it this far."

"It's been seven years since we last met," Khalil said softly.

My heart stirred as a vague memory worked its way up from the shadows of my past. And then I knew. My hand flew to my mouth and his expression changed.

"Leila," he said quickly, "I owe you my deepest apology. I will never forgive myself for letting that policeman take you, that day in Essaouira. I might have fought the man, diverted his attention so you could run —"

"No," I broke in. "You and your cousins did all you could to help me, but I would never have run. You see, in my heart and mind I was still a slave. It is I who must thank you for risking arrest to protect me."

"Well," he said quietly, "every road has two directions. I could not help you in Essaouira. I hope to change that, now." He withdrew a small, leather-bound book. "We have much to do, and precious little time."

"I don't understand —"

"Leila," Walid said softly, "Khalil is our attorney. He prepared the documents for the tearoom."

"I doubt you remember," Khalil explained, "but I was returning to Casablanca that evening seven years ago to prepare for my exams. Fatima and Aisha knew you'd be safe if I could get you to Amin's bookstore."

"I was so frightened, I barely understood anything," I replied.

"Since that time, I've completed my studies and earned an additional qualification in immigration law. I've learned as much about your situation as possible from Walid and Fatima. Now, if you agree, please tell me everything you can about what happened at the police station this past January."

Khalil took notes while, in a low voice, I described my arrest and interrogation. He was particularly interested in the woman Magistrate who sought medical care for me when I became ill in her office.

"The original charges against you include the undated theft of several unspecified rings, and a bracelet," he remarked. "This is hardly enough to imprison someone. Tell me, Leila: has anyone since the Magistrate discussed these charges with you?"

"No."

"Have any police or detectives been here since you were admitted to the hospital?"

"I don't think so."

"Has that woman at the door ever tried to interrogate you?"

"We've spoken on occasion," I admitted, glancing guiltily at Walid. "She belongs to the Minister."

"*Belongs?*" Khalid and Fatima echoed.

"I think I was purchased to replace her in the house. She remains his servant, to this day."

"That would explain why she looks half-starved," Fatima observed.

"And why she never leaves," Walid added.

"If this was a legitimate case," Khalil said, "the police would have kept you in custody, and when you required medical attention, they'd have taken you to a prison facility. Being held in a public hospital, but separated from other patients by this ridiculous curtain —" he shook it with contempt "— suggests that because you have a husband and family, the Minister is reluctant to simply make you disappear."

"Perhaps that was his original intention," Fatima observed, "until the police injured you so badly. Thank god that Magistrate, whoever she was, had the decency to send you here."

"And that your doctor," Walid added quietly, "has the courage to protect you from your accusers."

Involuntarily my eyes fell to my belly.

Khalil returned to his notes. "Now that the Minister has added to the original charges —"

"— More charges?" I asked, even as Walid shot him a warning look.

"She has the right to know," Fatima replied.

"She doesn't need to worry —" Walid began.

"— Please, Walid," I said. "I want to know everything."

Anger flooded his gaze, though when he spoke, his voice was restrained. "I believe this is a mistake, but do continue."

"According to the police," Khalil explained, "the Minister now says you also assaulted his blind mother, who was in fragile health. They claim your attempt to escape, by pretending to be married to a man you'd just met, is proof of your guilt."

"If you're arrested and convicted of these crimes," Fatima added quietly, "the Minister asks that you serve your sentence under house arrest in Essaouira."

"He could hold me there?"

"Unfortunately," Khalid said, "it's possible."

"But the law —"

"Some people think he *is* the law."

"We'll never allow this to happen," Walid insisted, placing his hand on my shoulder.

"I have a suggestion," Fatima said. "If you agree, Leila, Walid can bring you a small tape recorder, and if you can find even a few private minutes each day, we'll get the truth on record. I'll publish your story in my magazine."

"Who would care?"

"More people than you imagine. We have readers throughout North Africa and France."

"But what if this makes things worse?"

"We'll change the names, of course, but the Minister and his son will know you're capable of identifying them, if necessary. This story will serve as a warning that they can be exposed for everything they've done."

"Remember," Walid said, "when you lived with them you could barely read, and you couldn't write. You spoke Arabic poorly and knew no French. You were hungry, exhausted and forced to live with daily abuse."

"They believe you're still their slave," Fatima said. "They expect you to think, react, and fear them like a slave. But they have no idea who you are, Leila. When you were a nail you endured their blows, but now you're a hammer, and you must strike back."

"I agree with everything you've said," I replied. "I'm finally ready to tell the world what happened to me during my years in Essaouira."

Late in the evening, after the nurses sent the visitors home, the ward had a "quiet hour" before the lights went out. Patients talked to each other about medicine and pain, doctors and treatments, or told stories about family members, both the favored few who came to visit, or the greatly disliked, who did not.

Though I could not see the other patients because of the curtain drawn around my bed, I heard their blended voices, and knew this hour was a gift from god.

Tala was so focused on taking a portion of the food Selina and Hania brought for me each day, she never imagined a cache of *dinars* was growing beneath the drawer in my bedside table, next to the chair where she sat with me throughout the night.

Nor did she think to examine the pack of cigarettes in the pocket of Walid's jacket. Once he was seated close beside me, he removed a device that resembled a lighter. Without speaking, he held it close to his lips, pushed a button on the side, and a tiny red light flickered. Pushing the button a second time, he turned it off.

"Return it to me every morning," he whispered, "and I'll bring it back during my evening visit."

Those were the only words we ever exchanged about Fatima's article. If Walid was concerned I would endanger his mother and sister by revealing they had protected a fugitive, he said nothing. If he felt I dishonored our marriage by admitting to the world I'd been raped, he remained silent.

Over the following days, however, he sometimes paused at the curtain and gazed at me with a mixture of admiration and sadness. I realized, then, that he must have been listening to the tapes. I knew he was learning things about me that, despite everything I'd told him, he'd never suspected.

And as I spoke about my mountain village, the house of pleasure and my years inside the home of the Minister,

I found that instead of feeling ashamed of my ignorance and fear, I experienced a surging pride in my survival.

The morning after he took the tape for the last time, Walid returned with an unsigned card written in a handsome script: "*Cherished sister, I am happy to receive your news, and will pass it on to the rest of our family.*"

Though Tala inspected the card carefully before allowing Walid to share it with me, I knew she couldn't read it. I also knew it promised me a voice they would never extinguish, even if they silenced me with death.

The drone of the sonogram nearly drowned out Dr. Mansouri's endless chatter. Pleased that I'd walked the length of the hospital corridor several times with the aid of a cane, he advised me to exercise my hip as much as possible. "This is critically important after lying in bed for so many weeks. Are you still experiencing discomfort?"

"It's much better," I answered truthfully. "When do you plan to discharge me?"

"Very soon," he replied, eyes fixed on the screen. Without another word, he moved the sensor over my belly. "We won't worry about that, now. Let's see what your little one is doing."

I peered at the screen, expecting to see little more than the usual vague images that appeared when he scanned my hip and shoulder. Now I watched as uncertain waves shifted back and forth across the screen.

Listening to the electronic *whoosh-whoosh* of the sonogram, my attention wandered back to the strangeness of standing, after months of lying on my back. The whole

world seemed unbalanced, and the nurses who helped me
to my feet laughed at my unsteadiness, but —

"Ah...listen to the strength of that heartbeat." Dr.
Mansouri smiled. "You can really hear it, now!"

An oval balloon, shaped like a warped, clear soap bubble
appeared in the center of the screen. Inside this balloon lay
a small figure with a perfectly shaped head. The face was still
a sketch, but I could see with certainty that the baby's thumb
was in its mouth. The heartbeat rapped like a tiny drum.

"There," Dr. Mansouri murmured. "What, Madame,
do you think of that?"

Unwilling to weep, I chose not to speak. I stared at the
image of my baby, the baby that gave me the strength to
fight, and held back my tears.

"Let's see," he continued. "It appears you're now between seventeen and eighteen weeks along. The baby's
eyes are open, and she — or he — can blink. You see the
fingers? Can you count them? Look at those tiny toes!"

The *whoosh-whoosh* seemed to speed up.

"The baby receives nourishment from your body
through that long cord. The baby may be sleeping, now,
but soon you should feel it move. When you do, it will
probably feel like a tickling sensation. Most women say
they enjoy it very much."

Still staring wordlessly at the screen, I tried to take it all in.

"Perhaps the next time we look, the baby will decide
to let you see whether you're having a boy or a girl. Of
course, if you prefer not to know, I'll keep it a secret!"

The doctor continued to move the sensor over the rest
of my stomach, his eyes never leaving the screen. At last,
he turned it off.

I had neither moved nor spoken. I was scarcely breathing.

"The baby is very handsome, Leila. Everything looks perfectly normal, and the baby's size is good. There are no other masses, signs of fibroids, or other obstructions in or near the womb. In other words, this seems to be a very healthy pregnancy."

He picked up a paper towel and wiped the gel from my belly. "Do you have any questions?"

"When will they be able to see?" I asked quietly.

He sighed and leaned forward. "Some women never get very big during their pregnancy. You've gained some weight — I would like to see you gain a bit more — but it's possible most people won't notice, as long as you're wearing loose robes. However," he added, "do not avoid eating to hide what's happening in your body. It's very important that you remain healthy."

He considered me for a moment. "Leila, it's time you spoke to your husband."

"I know," I agreed.

"Now that it appears the baby is healthy, is there some other reason you're keeping your pregnancy secret?"

"Walid is already so worried about the police, my guard, and my recovery, I thought adding the baby to his concerns would only make matters worse."

"I don't like being part of this deception," Doctor Mansouri said. "Remember, the child is his, too."

"You've done me a great service by honoring my request," I replied. "Now I will respect yours. I'll share my news with Walid as soon as I can."

Tala's odor of sweat and sickness wafted around the curtain, even before I heard the swish of her robes. There was little movement, but I knew she was there, watching.

"Your doctor's joy is your deepest secret," she announced, derisively.

Annoyed, I answered before considering my words. "Why must you always speak in riddles?"

"Why do you think you can hide?"

"Tala, you sit beside me and hear my voice. How can you think me hidden?"

"I know what the others do not," she said. "I hear him speaking to the nurses, though his voice is low. He is proud of himself, your doctor — proud that you survived your injuries, proud of his brother-in-law's talents and proud that you have managed to keep your chi—"

"I know nothing of what you speak!"

"You think of nothing else," she purred, her voice now baiting. "And what else should you think of, when nothing else matters as much?"

She laughed spitefully.

"It feels like a victory, does it not? As if despite all they do to destroy you, something of you might survive."

This was no question; it was a statement of truth, and one that I, too, was just beginning to understand.

"Now you have something truly worth fighting for," she said, leaning closer to my face. "Something truly your own. Everything changes when you become a mother."

"Did he — did your son grow up there, in Essaouira?" I whispered, desperately trying to turn the conversation away from my baby. "Did your son grow up with his brother?"

"His brother?" she laughed, foul breath swirling around me. "His *brother?*"

Shaking her head, she peered at her hands, clawed and twisted with age. "We were sent to Agadir, where I worked in the home of the Minister's sister. She was not easy to please, but she was occupied with her businesses and, at least, did not strike me like her mother."

I swallowed, seeking words to bridge the distance between us.

"So you had your son beside you, there, in Agadir?"

"My Mistress' house is large, and there was always much work to be done, but I saw him most days."

"And — and he had the chance to go to school?"

"Yes, she sent him to school, though it ended when he was old enough for the army."

"But his father — the Minister — made sure he became an officer, and —"

"Yes," she cut in abruptly. "My son was protected, though he does not know the truth of his blood."

"He doesn't know the Minister is his father?"

"Of course not."

"But at least he knew you were his mother —"

She was silent a long time. When she spoke her voice was hollow.

"The Minister's sister had no children. She told my son he was an orphan, and brought him into her house as her own."

"Oh, Tala," I whispered.

"He had a far better life than I could have given him."

"And now, do you ever see him?"

"He sees no need to visit his 'mother's' dying servant," she replied with quiet bitterness. "Death is the black camel that kneels at every door. I am nothing more to him than the woman who cleaned the bedchambers, cooked the food and washed their clothes. Why would he have any interest in me?"

14. THE VOICE

Doctor Mansouri found me in the hospital garden, cane in my left hand, a nurse sitting on my right. I was now able to make my way through the hospital with ease. Wearing new leather slippers and a clean, midnight blue *djellaba* — gifts from Selina to replace my soiled and bloodied robes — I rested on a bench beneath a scarlet bougainvillea, enjoying the cool, early evening.

"Madame al-Magrihbi!" the doctor called out, causing several patients to turn and stare. "I'm delighted to see you forcing our nurse to get some exercise!"

I laughed along with the nurse. Dr. Mansouri escorted me back toward the hospital door.

"Your husband is here, and since he's not allowed to enter the garden, I offered to come and get you."

Still talking as he pulled back the curtain, we found Walid waiting. Though his face was composed, I saw both worry and excitement in his eyes. The two men helped me into a chair. Walid took a bright red magazine from his bag. A woman's face, head wrapped in a scarf, was shown in silhouette. Beneath the name of the magazine, *The Voice*, were the words, *Once a Slave, Never Truly Free*.

"What is this?" the doctor inquired.

"I believe," I answered calmly, "it's the story of my life."

Dr. Mansouri picked up the magazine and began reading, in a muted voice, aloud: "This is the true story of a girl taken by unknown men, at twelve years old, from her home in the Atlas Mountains.

"Driven across the country to the coastal city of Essaouira, the girl was sold to a brothel to pay her father's gambling debts. There she labored in the brothel kitchen until the owner, a woman, dressed her in women's garments and made her perform for guests.

"Soon sold again, this child, still too young to legally work in Morocco, found herself the property of a prominent judge. For the next decade she was forced to cook, clean and care for an elderly blind woman. She was also the victim of ongoing brutality at the hands of another servant, and suffered years of sexual abuse by the judge's adult son —"

Dr. Mansouri's voice faded.

I met his eyes without speaking. He returned to the magazine, now reading more quickly.

"The following pages will recount the details of this young woman's life, and in her own words, describe how she escaped her enslavement and struggled to build a new existence. Today recovering from a brutal beating by agents of her captors, this woman, who was once a slave, is still not truly free —

"— Are these the people who've accused you of theft?" he asked, interrupting himself again.

"Leila was held for nearly half her life, "Walid said. "Now, for the reasons you've just read, they're planning to take her again."

The doctor sank gingerly to the edge of the bed. When he spoke again, his voice was hushed.

"Who is responsible for putting this in a magazine?"

"Leila is not without friends," Walid answered, "but it would be better if they remain unnamed."

"Clearly," the doctor agreed. He looked at the magazine. "You realize this man will certainly react to this."

"We hope he'll be moved to leave Leila in peace."

"On the contrary," Dr. Mansouri said. "I predict he'll be enraged. Even if his name is not given, there are details in this article that will make his identity relatively easy to discover. I suspect he'll respond swiftly and without mercy. After all, he clearly feels he answers to no one."

Walid turned to me, unease in his eyes. "Fatima brought this copy to the tearoom today. It goes on sale the day after tomorrow."

Dr. Mansouri's eyes followed Walid's gaze. "Surely your guard sees you're walking now, Madame. I've done all I can to protect you, but I think your time of safety here is finished."

"She searched me when I came in," Walid remarked. "It's fortunate she didn't look closely at the magazine."

"It wasn't luck," I said. "She can't read."

The doctor stood. "I can discharge you tomorrow, Madame, but you must first have somewhere safe to go."

"We will keep Leila safe," Walid responded, also rising. "Once she leaves the hospital, they will never find her again."

"You'll have to move fast, and I think—" the doctor glanced from my stomach to my face. I nodded, an understanding passing between us.

"I'll begin the paperwork," he continued. "Early tomorrow morning I'll have you taken to another part of the hospital for tests. It would be best if someone waited with a car at the rear loading dock at, say, six in the morning. Your mother can come to the ward with her usual gift of food for the nurses, and while your guard is helping herself to the pastries and bread, Leila can be helped into the car. It will take some time for your guard to realize you haven't returned. The nurses will tell her, truthfully, that you were sent to another part of the hospital, which will buy you a bit more time to get away."

"What will happen to you, Dr. Mansouri?"

"I'll tell your guard that the nurse who brought you downstairs left you alone in a bathroom, and when she returned, you had disappeared. I'll have absolutely no idea where you might be."

He reached for my hands.

"I have never treated anyone quite like you, Leila. Your strength and courage have been an inspiration. You'll have to be careful in the next few weeks, however. A fall could be disastrous for your —" he paused — "recovery. I hope you'll find a way to let me know about your continued progress."

He held my eyes a moment longer. Then he grasped Walid's hand, pulled him into a brief hug, and vanished.

"The article is very powerful," Walid said as he sank down beside me. "No one who reads it will doubt every word is true."

"Please thank Fatima for me."

"Tomorrow you'll thank her, yourself."

Walid reached in his pocket and produced a small blue box. "I had planned to wait for a happier occasion," he added, handing the box to me, "but this might bring us luck in the morning."

Inside lay a simple gold band, not unlike the wedding ring that vanished when I was in police custody.

"When you're safe, we'll look for something nicer," he said as he placed it on my finger. "For now, just remember how much I love you."

He stood and smiled, calm determination in his eyes. "I should turn in early tonight. I have a very important delivery to make in the morning. I'll leave this copy of the magazine with you, but be sure to keep it away from curious eyes."

"Walid —!"

He turned, surprised at the urgency in my voice.

"Please, I need to speak to you before you go."

"Are you worried about tomorrow?" he asked, sitting again. "Everything will be fine."

"No," I said, "there's something else."

Though I had imagined this moment many times over the past few weeks, suddenly I found I couldn't speak. Reaching for his hands, I placed them tenderly on the center of my belly.

Slowly he met my gaze. He opened his mouth, then closed it, saying nothing.

"I found out a few weeks ago, but decided to tell no one until I was sure the baby survived."

"You mean —"

"Yes, *habib*, at the end of the summer you're going to be a father."

For the first time since I met Walid, every trace of sadness swept from his face, and elation flooded his eyes.

"You're pregnant?" he whispered.

"I am," I answered, "and the doctor says our baby's doing fine."

We stared at each other. Then, suddenly we both began to laugh. Walid laughed until, with tears in his eyes, he pulled me into his arms. We held each other in perfect stillness until someone flashed the lights, signaling that visiting hours were over.

"I can't wait to see Mother's face when we tell her, tomorrow," he said as he prepared to stand. "And Hania? Think of all the shopping she'll want you to do!"

"You must promise me something," I said, grasping his fingers as he stood. "If anything happens — if somehow, for some completely unexpected reason, I'm taken by Essaouira — promise me you'll protect our child."

"Nothing will —"

"*Promise me*," I repeated.

"You have my promise, Leila. But nothing is going to go wrong tomorrow."

Once alone, I sat on the edge of the bed, thinking. With the help of Khalil, Fatima, and Aisha, I could easily disappear in the vast sprawl of Casablanca, and never be found by the Minister.

Once hidden, however, I might never again enter our tearoom, return to my class, spend time with my friends, or — god forbid — live openly with Selina, or Walid.

I knew what it meant to hide. I'd spent much of my adult life in hiding. But now, with this new life to care for, I could no longer exist as a fugitive.

I had published my story in *The Voice* to protect the world I built with those I love. Not to end it.

Though unprepared for what I must do, there was no time to hesitate. Very quietly I opened the drawer of the bedside table and removed the roll of *dinars*. I placed the bills between the pages of the magazine, and slid the folded magazine into the inside pocket of my new *djellaba*.

And I waited.

During the hour that evening, I took a pen left behind by a nurse and, with many mistakes, wrote a letter to Walid on the inside cover of Aisha's book of poetry. I knew my actions would cause him heartache, but I believed my plan, if I succeeded, was the best way to protect us from the Minister.

When the lights went out, the beds fell silent, and the time of the vulture was upon me.

Concerned that she might appear at my bedside and keep me trapped until dawn, I carefully climbed from the bed and pushed my feet into my new slippers. Getting onto my feet was excruciating — but far less so than before my surgery. Shaking and sweating from the effort, I reached for my *djellaba* and my cane, and opened the curtain, moving as normally as my fragile legs allowed.

I looked neither left nor right. I knew that folded, clean clothing was kept in a cabinet near the door. The cabinet remained unlocked; I'd watched a nurse remove a kaftan from it only that morning.

I opened the cabinet and reached inside. A woman in a nearby bed coughed roughly. I did not pause in my search. A nurse, after all, would do no less.

I removed an armful of garments, and, leaning on my cane for support, took a foal's steps toward the door. In daylight the nurses often gathered at a counter outside, bringing newspapers, files and medicines to the supervisors seated at desks in the rear of the station.

I had never ventured beyond the ward at night, and had no idea whether I'd be met by two, or twenty nurses. And of course, I fully expected to find Tala on one of the benches beyond the door. This risk I was prepared to face, having no other plan.

The door to the ward had a large window of tempered, wavy glass that permitted light, but not the gaze of outsiders, to fall upon the patients. I pressed my face against the glass, searching for some sign of movement.

There was none. I pushed the door open a few inches and found the nurses' station deserted. Slowly, hardly moving, I limped through the door and heard it swish close behind me.

Now my heart thumped wildly. I had nothing in my possession but an armful of stolen clothes, and the *dinar*-filled magazine. To some, I would have appeared ridiculous, but escaping with little more than my hope had saved me before.

I moved toward the nearest exit, intending to change into my new attire as quickly as I could. As I made my way down the hall, gritting my teeth against the pain, I heard voices behind me.

I didn't stop or look back. The voices gathered at the nurses' station, then burst into relaxed laughter. I reached the end of the hall and slipped into the dim light of the narrow, airless stairwell. I didn't know how long I'd have before someone noted my absence, nor how hard anyone, except Tala, would try to find me.

But I didn't want them to call Walid and Selina, in the middle of the night, to report that I was missing. I hoped my husband and his mother would learn of my disappearance only when they arrived the next morning. I prayed Selina would find the book, there, on the bedside table, and give it to Walid.

It was difficult to remove my patient's gown, and even more difficult to button the white blouse and long black skirt I had taken from the cabinet, and to get back into the hooded *djellaba* Selina had given to me. The skirt and *djellaba* were made of heavy, good-quality fabric, and because they were large, did much to hide my belly. While not expensive clothing, anyone who saw me would believe

I worked in a school or hospital. The only truly unusual thing was my cane and hesitant gait.

My hair had grown several inches and now hung in a fuzzy half-braid to my shoulders. Quickly I covered it with my hood. Steadying myself with my free hand on the bannister, I began my miserable descent, eyes fixed on the steps beneath my feet, weight balanced on the cane.

I had just reached the bottom when I heard the door open and close above me. Footsteps quickly mounted the staircase and another door opened. Again the stairwell fell silent.

Sweat broke out on my forehead. I steeled myself for what lay ahead. And then I heard the hoarse voice.

"So, the night is the mother of plots."

I turned to find Tala's misshapen shadow blocking my way out of the hospital.

"I must go, Mother."

"You must stay." She moved a step closer. Her eyes glittered in the low light.

"I cannot stay, Tala. You know why."

She grunted and moved even closer. Strangely, I was not aware of her odor. I thought only of my pounding heart, and the tiny heart beating beside it.

"When he learns of the child, you will be even more valuable to him."

"We have no value, you and I," I replied, leaning heavily upon the bannister. "To him, we are only possessions, like a shoe or a chair."

"Yet he has given us our lives —"

"He took our lives away," I countered, struggling to steady my voice.

"What would you have been in your mountain village?"

"What was I in your Master's home? Both were a kind of death for me."

I straightened my back. "I must go, Mother, and you must open the way for me."

"You know I cannot."

"I know you can — and you will."

She might have laughed — the sound was strangled, deep, anguished, and amused.

"And what will happen to me?" she asked, and there was honesty in her question.

"For the first time in your life, you will know what freedom feels like."

"My Master will punish me."

"Nothing is certain but the unforeseen."

"And what will happen to my son?"

I paused, considered, then replied gently, "He does not know you as his mother, Tala. If he is loved by our Master's sister, she will protect him."

Now it was she who paused. "My Master will want your child, too."

"Then I must become the thief they accuse me of being. I will steal myself, my child, and our future."

The ache in my hip flamed across my back and lower body; I had not stood for so long in months. Still, Tala remained in the doorway, grasping the edges of her *djellaba* with her gnarled hand.

"Why should you have freedoms he never gave me? You are not the only one who knows pain." In a swift movement she released the robe she'd held, night and day, so close to her face.

A deep gouge ran from Tala's forehead to the base of her chin, maiming the left side of her face.

"Hassan knew his work," she said quietly. "We are more alike than you know."

"Mother," I whispered. I reached out and lifted a steady hand toward her face. She flinched as I touched the deep cut, drawing my fingers gently from her eyes to her chin.

"What is your name?" I asked.

"You know it."

"What is your name?" I repeated, still touching her skin. Wetness appeared in her eyes, wandering slowly down the cavern, toward my thumb.

"Please, I said very quietly. "Tell me your name."

"Nadia," she whispered.

I took her into my arms and held her. I don't know how long we huddled in the dim silence of the stairwell. I only know I could no longer smell her odor of death as she shook in my arms.

Finally I spoke. "Come, Nadia. The night grows late."

She stepped back and held my gaze. Then, without another word, she moved aside.

The door of the hospital opened to a blue-black night heavy with the perfume of early summer blossoms and the promise of rain. I filled my lungs with the scents of freedom, and made my way to the street, where a row of taxis waited, engines throbbing. Though I had ridden in a taxi only once in my life — on my wedding night — I remembered that Walid had simply given the man our destination, and soon we'd arrived.

I did the same, marveling at the speed with which we passed through the empty streets, neon blurring, and bed sheets, hung from balconies, billowing ghostly in the humid breeze.

The car stopped at a curb alongside many other taxis, and I took some *dinars* from the magazine folded inside my *djellaba*. Though no one had ever told me, I reasoned that he would expect a tip, and I added a few *dinars* to the cost of the journey.

Hobbling, holding my jaw tight against the pain, I crossed a wide intersection and entered the station. Approaching the window with determination that vanquished my fear, I purchased a ticket for the next bus to Essaouira.

15. THE WHITE SALON

The road from Casablanca to Essaouira follows routes as ancient as the travels of mankind. Born at the sea, it passes through a city made rich from the merchant trade — Marrakech — then plunges south toward the timeless portal of the mighty Sahara.

I would not have known how to find my way back, had I not listened so closely to the guests in our tearoom, who often spoke of their travel by bus to visit family members in Marrakech, or their trips through Essaouira while en route to Agadir.

Now, riding on a bus for the first time, I marveled at the smooth certainty of the road, as Casablanca surrendered to goat-riddled fields splattered with poppies and waving golden flowers. Pressing my face against the window, from time to time I saw a village of mud brick dwellings emerge from violet-blue hills, the children running barefoot behind us as their mothers, swaddled in black, sat straight-backed on plastic chairs outside their doors. Each village was crowned by a minaret, reaching skyward to god.

I will always remember the mules pulling carts of hay, and the camels gathered beside their white-cloaked masters, as we entered a valley and were suddenly besieged by the desert. The sand glittered like sugar beneath the late noon sun, melting, in the distance, into the red-humped mountains of my birth.

We rolled into Marrakech at noon. The city was as I remembered it from years before, when Walid drove me here with Selina. Modern hotels crouched along the outskirts, and the houses aged as we gained the center. Lanterns hung from whitewashed terraces, and street musicians roamed the great square, alive with tourists. The wide boulevards were pillared with orange trees, now glowing like tiny bright orbs against their waving green leaves.

Exhausted, but resolved, I limped across the street from the bus station and entered a small cafe. The proprietress, a large woman in a lime green *takchita*, looked me over carefully before gesturing toward a table.

I ate a simple meal of yogurt and lentils. The waiter was too concerned with tourists to pay much attention to me. When I returned to the bus station, limping badly, I boarded my next bus, took my seat and tried to rest.

My hand felt heavy with the weight of my new ring. Though my heart longed to hear Walid's voice and to soothe his fears, I knew my guilt for causing him yet more fear might turn me away from my purpose. I thought of the words I had scrawled inside the poetry book, and the cruelty of telling him, in this way, that I had taken it upon myself to set us all free:

> *Cherished husband,*
> *Please do not follow me to Essaouira. I am doing what I must for us all.*
> *If I do not return, do everything you can to find our child.*
> *Please thank Selina and Hania for their great kindness to me.*
> *I love you.*
> *Leila*

Though he would be deeply distressed, I hoped he would understand that I sought to spare him more fear and sorrow. Armed with Tala's confession, and the information shared by Fatima and Khalil, I understood that my Master and his son intended to return me to Essaouira, where I would remain trapped, for what was left of my life, in the house above the sea.

More than a mere servant, I served a crucial purpose in that house: keeping me starved, beaten, ignorant and hopeless, would remind their most valuable possession — Young Mistress — how lucky she was *not* to be me.

The road that departed Marrakech was bordered with rich shades of green. Herds lounged in the distance, and black birds wheeled overhead. I felt a tickling and placed my hands inside my robe, where I could gently rub my belly. I said a prayer, then murmured a lullaby, even as the bus passed a young woman with a baby tied to her chest and a small boy at her side. The sky cooled to a silvery blue; the afternoon light was softer here, than in Casablanca.

I did not dwell on this, nor on what would happen when I arrived at my destination.

I could only think of our child.

I smelled the city long before I saw it. The fishermen's boats already drifted homeward, sitting low on the tide as they entered the harbor. The white walls ringed their soaring spires, and there, before me, was the gate. Women were seated before the tall arch, grills sending up wraiths of sweet smoke, baskets of scarlet flowers at their feet.

As the bus swept into the city, I was astounded by how small and provincial it seemed, compared to Casablanca. Though the walls of the fortress still stood sentinel against enemies from centuries before, the noise of the streets seemed a whisper against the roar of my new home. I thought of my fear when I crept through the *souk* of Essaouira, and how easily I became lost. Never did I dream the whole of this city could fit into a few blocks of Casablanca.

Descending the bus steps with care, I stood in the center of Essaouira's most important boulevard. Head down, guided by instinct, I moved forward on uncertain legs. I felt myself observed, assessed, judged by every stranger I passed. The *souk* was full of women in black or dark blue robes, but my gait, clumsy on the cane, made me even more visible.

"You are alone?" a man inquired, and I looked up to find a smile curling over brown teeth.

I turned away. His eyes fell to my swollen middle, and he melted back into the crowd.

I had no time to consider which streets to take, nor the safest or fastest route. I approached the damp passage, and found it looked exactly as it had seven years before, when I slipped from the house while Hassan slept. My heart beat wildly, and I felt a stirring in my belly. What if the Master was there? What if Hassan met me at the door? What if Young Master waited — as he waited in my nightmares — embittered wife by his side?

Steps faltering, I leaned against the wall opposite the front door of the house of Yusef Hakim Senhaji, former Magistrate of Essaouira, now Minister of Justice for the nation of Morocco.

Though nauseated, I took several deep breaths and straightened my back. I had to finish the journey that began the day I put on Young Mistress' clothes and fled, so many years before.

Forcing myself to think of nothing, I grasped the brass knocker and struck the door.

For many seconds there was no sound. I waited, heart slamming against my ribs. I lifted the knocker and struck the door again.

Now there were footsteps. Quick, but hesitant. Light, but not those of a small child. An eye appeared at a peep-hole I had never been quite tall enough to use. I emptied my face of all emotion and waited, looking directly at the door.

Moments passed. Just as I again reached for the knocker, the door opened a crack.

"Peace be with you," a voice whispered. I knew this could not be Hassan.

"And also with you," I answered.

"You would like something?" the person asked, still speaking quietly.

"Please," I said. "May I step inside?"

Again, there was hesitation. Then the door swung open and, drawing in my breath, I entered the courtyard. Everything had changed, yet all was the same. Lovely aqua tiles ringed the small octagonal fountain, which still flowed with a soothing murmur. Stairs ascended to the second story — how well I knew them! — but the flowering jasmine and orange trees in the atrium were much thicker and taller.

Though my forehead was suddenly damp, I pushed back my fear, breathing the perfume of the bright blossoms. Slowly I regarded my host.

I faced a child — a boy, in fact, of uncertain age. His very black hair was cut so close it was but a shadow on his scarred scalp. Dressed in a soiled, oversized burnoose, his rubber sandals were too large for his dirt-caked feet. He stood beside the door as if ready to dodge a blow. Fear lived in his hooded eyes.

"I am Madame al-Maghribi Leila," I said in a quiet voice. "Is your Master at home?"

"The Minister is in the capital," he replied, his voice low.

"And your Young Master?" I asked evenly.

He shook his head in quick, slashing motions. "He is away from home this afternoon."

I flushed at those words. I had hoped against all reason that perhaps, just perhaps, he might still be abroad, though I knew no jungle is without a serpent.

"Perhaps your Mistress is present?" I continued politely.

"The Mistress?"

"The mistress who cannot see."

He looked confused at my words, and lowered his face to think. "I do not know this person," he answered. "Are you sure she lives here?"

"She did some years ago," I answered. "I have not visited the family for some time." I looked toward the stairs. "Is your Young Mistress at home? It is she I came to see."

He looked me over furtively, judging the fabric of my *djellaba*. I knew that while such clothing was not special for Casablanca, many women would have been happy for this robe in Essaouira.

"My Mistress is sleeping," he answered. "Can you come back later?"

"I would rather wait," I said. "Do you think she will sleep much longer?"

He shook his head. "She is going out tonight, so I think she will soon rise." He paused, weighing what he should do next. Again his dark eyes took in my clothes. Timidly, he looked into my face for the first time. I don't know what he saw in my eyes, but he raised his arm and said in an uncertain voice, "If you like, you may wait in the white salon. I will bring you tea."

I followed the boy into the house above the sea. Fearful of my memories, I willed myself to look neither left, nor right, as we made our way through the double doors.

Carefully, as if I were sitting in a room spun from the clouds, I placed myself where I would never have dared when I lived in that house — squarely in the center of a pure white divan, bathed in light pouring in through round, blue-glass windows. In my day, the white salon was opened only for guests of prominence, but it was clear that since Young Mistress' arrival, the room was in regular use.

A pair of gold leather sandals lay abandoned near an armchair, and a shawl of fine aqua wool was tossed over one of the sofas. Magazines littered the floor, and a large television now graced one of the Egyptian mother-of-pearl cabinets. The salon smelled of sweet lemon and gardenia, a fragrance I sometimes caught in the hair of Frenchwomen, when they bent over our display cases in the tearoom.

I peered at the magazines, curious about what might interest Young Mistress. Most were about fashion, and were written in French. One, however, had a bright red cover bearing the silhouette of a woman in a headscarf. Had Fatima sent her a copy?

The door opened behind me and the boy brought in a teak tray I knew well. On it he balanced a small silver samovar and two slender glasses, hand-painted with wandering vines. A fine dish bore three butter *ghoribas*. He set the tray on a side table and bent low to pour the tea.

"Thank you," I said quietly. "I will wait a few more minutes before drinking or eating."

He quickly straightened and stood beside me, the blue light from the window staining his face. I saw his eyes move toward the sweets, so I reached over and offered him one. Again he shook his head, the motion suggesting many years of training about eating food meant for those in a higher station. Rarely had I enjoyed my own cooking while living in this house. When I escaped, I had been close to starving, though I'd spend hours preparing food every day.

"Where do you come from?" I asked in a conversational voice. His gaze grew distant, and he hesitated before answering.

"Agadir."

"I'm told it is a lovely city," I responded. He remained silent.

"Were you in service in another house?"

He paused, and then nodded once.

"Have you been in Essaouira a long time?"

His eyes darted toward mine, then again settled on the plate of *ghoribas*. He gave a small shrug that might have meant he didn't know — or that he no longer cared.

"Essaouira is a very pretty city, too, isn't it?"

Again he shrugged.

"How did you come to be here?" I asked, watching him closely.

"The Minister's sister," he whispered, his voice trailing off.

"Yes," I replied, "I met her many years ago, when she came for a wedding. Did she bring you here?"

"No. She told my mother I could come here and go to school."

"That was very kind. Do you like school?"

Again he fell silent. I looked at his dirty robes and shaved scalp. I considered his fear. And I knew he'd never been to school. He had probably never been permitted to leave the house.

"Do you — do you ever think about going home?" I asked, feeling intense sadness.

Now he stared at his feet. I wondered what they'd done to break him, as I had been broken. I wondered what secrets lay beneath his robes.

"What is your name, child?"

"Ayrad," he said without raising his eyes.

"Ayrad," I repeated. "What a beautiful Berber name! You are named after the king of all beasts," I said gently, "the strongest, biggest and most noble hunter in all the world. He is brave and powerful, and fears nothing. Like him, you must be brave, child. You must do whatever is necessary to be safe. Do you understand?"

He looked up, his black eyes searching mine. I saw his chest rising and falling beneath the burnoose, and his little hands closed into fists.

"Now, go," I said. "I can pour the tea myself. And take the *ghoribas*. You have my permission to eat them, if you'd like."

His was gone in an instant, and I rose, keenly aware that these might have been the only kind words he'd heard since leaving home.

I walked slowly to the center of the room and closed my eyes against the images that came flooding back: images of beatings, blood, pain. Words that wounded as much as fists. Fear that crippled even more than the blows.

No, I thought, *I will not become that battered, terrified child again.* Not now. Not ever.

And I heard it — the soft, insistent, swelling, rising and falling, rushing forward and back, murmuring, laughing, living, breathing sea.

"Who let you in here?"

She stood before me in a mint silk *kaftan*, golden hair loose on her shoulders. A telephone lay in her open, pink-nailed hand. She had been preparing to call someone when she walked into the room.

"You have no right to be in this house."

"I have come to speak to you," I answered, as calmly as my racing heart would allow.

"You've come — to speak to *me*? You bitch — you should get on your knees and beg me not to call the police!"

"I will not try to stop you," I said, "but before they arrive, I will ask you to listen to what I've traveled so far to say."

She might have made good on her threat, had her curiosity not been stronger than her outrage. She measured me — the rough curls escaping my braid, my simple blue *djellaba*, the cane and my uneven gait — and her eyes settled on my scar.

"So it *was* you in the tearoom that day."

"It's strange," I answered. "I lived in fear of you for so long, I could barely go out on the streets. And suddenly you were there, just in front of me, and I wasn't afraid at all."

"If you hadn't broken the law, you'd have nothing to fear," she replied with heat.

To my surprise, I laughed. My laughter began softly, with pity, but as I looked at her fine-boned, unblemished skin, perfect lips and bright eyes, I became even more amused by her absurd and willful blindness.

"You find this funny, you savage cow?"

"No, I find it sad."

"You're a thief —"

"Yes," I confessed, "I once stole a beautiful turquoise tunic, a pair of white pants, a silk headscarf, sunglasses and a pair of leather sandals."

"You also stole jewelry —"

"Your jewelry is safely locked away, and I have neither seen, nor ever touched it."

Strangely, she didn't deny this. I knew she was trying to decide whether anyone might believe me over her. Her eyes swept the room, and her gaze fell on the magazine.

She took a step toward me. "I expect you'll also tell me you had nothing to do with the lies in that story?"

"Then you've seen it."

"Someone sent it here, and fortunately I found it before my husband or his father."

"I've told no lies."

"Every word of it is untrue. I know what kind of woman you are. I know you lived in a brothel. I know you tried to convince my husband to lie with you, then later claimed you were raped."

"Did he tell you this?"

"What does it matter? If you'd been honest you would never have run away!"

"I left to save my life."

"Ridiculous! Many people would be happy to live in the home of a man as important as my husband's father!"

"Let me show you such happiness," I said.

With these words, I did as Tala had done, knowing that flesh speaks what words cannot describe. Opening my blouse, I slipped off the straps of my bra and turned, exposing the gouges on my shoulders and spine.

I then faced her once more; she took in the ridges on my naked breasts, my collarbone, and the echo of the gash across my nose and cheek.

"Who did this?" she whispered.

"Hassan."

"Hassan is dead."

"May he rest in peace."

I put on my blouse and closed my *djellaba*. Her chest rose and fell, but she didn't speak.

"You weren't sure, that day in the tearoom," I said. "You truly didn't recognize me."

"It's been years, and you've changed so much —"

"And in the past you never really looked at me."

"Why should I have looked at a servant?"

"Seeing me as human might have stopped *you* from lying."

She looked up sharply. "Do you pretend you haven't lied? I know what really happened between you and my husband. I saw the child!"

"Child?"

"That child in the tearoom."

For the first time since she'd entered the white salon, I was struck dumb. I stared at her, trying to understand what she meant.

"*I — saw — the — child,*" she repeated, emphasizing every word. "He came out of the back as we were preparing to leave."

"The only children in the tearoom that day were my nephews."

"Don't lie to me, you bitch!" she exploded. "I know what went on in that room upstairs. My mother took one look at you, and even *she* knew!"

"Do you think," I said softly, "that I wished to be used like an animal for your husband's pleasure?"

"But you *are* an animal," she replied with venom. "Did you honestly think I wanted them to find you? You fool! I was *glad* when you vanished! Of course, once you were gone, he could think of nothing else."

She moved away from me and sank down on the white sofa, the silk *kaftan* billowing up around her.

"He's had agents as far away as Agadir looking for you. He was so obsessed that I thought —"

"— I must have been carrying his child."

"Naturally," she replied dully. "Why else would I ever think about an ugly, dirty, ignorant girl? I studied in France. I could have worked —"

Suddenly she fell silent, her memories of freedom rising like a wall between us.

"Now that you've seen my body," I asked, "do you doubt what I say is true?"

She looked away. "Then the boy in Casablanca is not his?"

"The boy is Casablanca is not his. I took nothing from this house except enough clothing to make the guards at the gate think I was —" I broke off and she looked back at me. "To make them think I was *you*."

We regarded each other without speaking. My eyes traveled over her handsome face, silken hair and bright blue gaze. I wondered what she saw when she looked at me.

"You're pregnant," she stated, eyes narrowing as she stared at my robe.

"I am," I replied in a clear voice, "and the father is a man who loves and honors me with his name."

A hush bloomed that lasted for seconds, then minutes. Beneath us I could hear the insistent, murmuring sea.

"He's here in Essaouira," she stated in a flat voice. "He will return soon. I'd leave if I were you."

"If you're truly the Mistress of this house, you must convince him to leave me, and my family, in peace."

"How can I do that?"

"Fight for the woman who studied in France. Fight for your own survival."

"You know nothing about my life."

"I'm not speaking now as a slave to her Mistress. I'm addressing you as one woman to another. You have no chance for happiness until he forgets me."

I managed to walk to the door without limping, then looked back. She had drawn the shawl tight around her body. Her gaze was fixed on the floor.

"I hate you," she murmured, without looking up.

"No," I replied. "You hate your husband. Just remember: you can leave him. *I did.*"

I paused. "There is one more thing. Send that child in your kitchen home."

Once outside the house the throbbing in my hip became unbearable. Still, I made my way along the mud path of the narrow passage, reaching up to touch the damp walls looming over me. I paused at the split in the street, remembering that distant morning when I first set foot outside the house after years of being held inside. The clouds had been low and dark, unlike this day, when the sky was a cloudless, searing blue. To the left I heard the sounds of traffic beckoning me to the crowded anonymity of the *souk*. To the right was the sea.

I emerged on the beach as I had done that first afternoon, nearly seven years before, when I abandoned my slavery and made a leap toward a new self. The sand was not as hot this day, for we had yet to reach midsummer, but the beach was deserted. A light wind sent gulls wheeling overhead, singing their pleasure in riding the sea's white foam.

In the distance I saw the figure of a small woman, wrapped in a *djellaba,* making her way across the sand. A mass of swaying fabric beneath the sun, she lifted her feet high to move her robe over the drifts. Behind her, waves leapt hard against the rocks. In her dark silhouette I found the image of my past, moving steadily away from me.

I walked toward the city, still thinking of the sea. Just as I reached the street I felt a warm tickling in my belly. Looking down, I placed my hands on my *djellaba* and my attention was drawn to my reflection in a puddle.

I stared at the face rippling gently in the mirror of the sky. The woman who looked back shifted between the strength of my mother, the kindness of Selina, the courage of Fatima and patience of Aisha, the boldness of Hania and the unending perseverance of a mountain girl known by many different names.

I realized with a start that I had grown from a bartered, battered child into a woman who walked alone to protect the people she loved.

A dark-haired man, eyes fixed on his mobile phone, bumped into me without excusing himself. I took a step back, struggling to keep my balance. He glanced at me, instantly taking in my *djellaba* and my cane. Standing tall, I looked squarely into his eyes.

He stared back for a moment, and finding me of no consequence, continued stabbing at his phone as he walked away. The acrid scent of his cologne wafted out behind him. I watched as he strode toward the passage and turned left at the split.

Still, I did not hurry. I knew she would not send him after me. Slowly, with as much determination as my hip allowed, I walked back through Essaouira to the station. A bus would leave for Casablanca within the hour. I would arrive late at night, but first I would call Walid, so he could be there to meet me.

Then, no matter what anyone thought, I would sleep in Walid's arms that night in our bed above the bakery, deep in the *souk* of Casablanca.

16. MOONLIGHT

My mother often said that a small stone props up the water jar.

The magazine featuring my story was published the day after I returned from Essaouira. Readers across the country and, indeed, in France, learned of my time as a slave in the Minister of Justice's home.

Though we all thought ourselves prepared for the worst, when the worst happened, we discovered we were not prepared at all.

No police came to our apartment in the *souk* to arrest me. None appeared at the door of our tearoom, either. Instead, the offices of *The Voice* were raided. Computers were taken and files confiscated. Fearing reprisal, Fatima was forced to flee the country. Aisha reported she was safe in France, but urged us to make no attempt to contact her, to protect her from discovery.

Fatima's colleagues at the magazine told the authorities they didn't know the identity of the woman whose story was told. I was, therefore, shielded from Fatima's fate. Though many copies of the magazine were sold in our country and abroad, neither the Moroccan television nor radio reported anything about the article. It seemed to vanish as quickly as it appeared.

We went on working, baking and serving our customers. Dr. Mansouri often came in at midday and, after his lentil soup, watched with pride as I moved more easily on my new hip. We spoke in muted tones about the vulture, who'd vanished the night I fled, and had not been seen again.

Five months later, cradled in the arms of Hania and Aisha, I pushed our daughter into Selina's waiting hands. She lifted the baby to the midwife, who examined her and returned her to me. The birth was perfect; I only wish that one of the women in that room could have been my mother.

Walid murmured thanks to god as he entered the room, then sank to the bed beside us.

A tiny fist emerged from the shawl and her fingers wrapped around his thumb. Her thick crop of hair was light brown, with whispers of gold at the temples. Her pouting lips were mirrors of Walid's and her satiny cheeks were dipped a dusty-rose.

"I've been thinking," he said softly, so as not to awaken our child, "that we might name her Tiziri."

"Yes," I agreed. "This was also in my thoughts. Thank you, Walid. My mother would be proud."

Al-Maghribi Zahra Tiziri's birth certificate identifies her parents as al-Maghribi Walid and al-Maghribi Zahra Leila. The certificate was registered by Walid, with Khalil as a witness, in our district of Casablanca two days after her birth. For me, this paper means the world. It is far easier to make a non-person disappear, and my child must survive.

Though I might have found many excuses to remain in our bed while Ziri was an infant, I returned to the tea-room as quickly as I could. We moved a small crib into the storage area, beside the bed where Hania's sons sometimes napped, and I brought Ziri to work with me. The pleasure I felt when pressing my hands into the warm dough did much to ease my fatigue during the first weeks after her birth. Everyone begged me to do less, but I had been in the hospital so long, I needed work more than words could express. Walid watched me closely, and said little.

I saw myself clearly in the baby's face, which was — as Bahia had described me long before — heart-shaped, with a tiny cleft chin and wide-set green eyes. A perfect blend of her parents, her skin settled on a tone lighter than mine and darker than her father's, which made her eyes seem even brighter. Her hair sprang out in heavy ringlets, with golden threads mixed in with the brown. Whether she was sleeping or awake, a steady stream of family and friends made their way to her little bed, sometimes just to gaze at her.

The letter arrived on a typical Thursday, as we were filling the display cases, and Selina chatting with customers.

The agent from the post office asked for the owner. Selina, Walid and I stopped our work and watched as he removed an envelope with "Official Document" stamped in red across the top, and asked one of us to sign for it. Though troubled, Selina went back to work and Walid took the letter into the storage room, where he had the privacy to read it.

When he came back into the bakery his expression was grave, so I set aside my bowl and walked out to the beach with him.

"They've finally acted," he said, handing the letter to me. "They've pressured the building owner not to renew our lease."

The letter was written in French, with many words and phrases I didn't know. "I don't understand," I said as I returned it to him.

"The letter informs us that this property is being re-zoned, and food can no longer be prepared or served on the premises."

"But we have a good relationship with the landlord."

"The landlord wants no problems with the authorities."

"But our customers love us —"

"Exactly," he said, looking out to sea.

"Then," I said with a falling heart, "this is the work of Essaouira."

"This is the work of Essaouira," Walid agreed. "I'll call Khalil and see what he can do."

"We'll have to tell Hania and Rachid."

"Yes. They should know."

"Should we tell Mother?"

He paused. "Not quite yet. It just might break her heart."

We returned to the kitchen, where Selina waited with a question in her eyes. I smiled and picked up the baby as Walid explained that the city wanted to rezone beachfront properties.

"Let's hear what Khalil thinks about this," Walid said as he returned the letter to the envelope.

Selina tipped her head slightly to the side, reading her son's face, but said nothing.

Khalil contacted the building owner, who claimed to know nothing of the source of the new restriction. The owner agreed we'd been excellent tenants, and that our tearoom provided a necessary service to the community. But he also said he would not risk problems with the authorities by refusing to respect the new restriction. In other words, we had three months — until the end of our current lease — to prepare to close.

Khalil followed the trail to the top officials in the city. The only explanation he received was that several vendors who owned booths along the beach had complained that the tearoom robbed them of customers. We knew this to be untrue, for the people who came to the tearoom were not interested in the grilled sausages, french fries and soft drinks sold elsewhere.

Walid and Khalil began looking for a new location for *Chez Selina*. After days of searching, we applied for leases on three businesses, and were refused as tenants each time. Our bank claimed that the balance owed on our loan on *Chez Selina* made us unfit for a new lease. We could not even secure the name of a government official with whom to register a complaint.

With only five weeks left, Walid and I sat down one evening in the rear of Amin's bookstore to discuss what must be done. Hania and Rachid joined us; Khalil and Aisha were there, too. Amin listened in between taking care of his customers.

"I wish," Khalil began, "that I had a way to break through the walls the judge and his son have created. Though they are indeed wealthy and powerful, I still believe if I could talk to the right person, we could do something to protect you."

"Even if you re-opened the old bakery, you'd never make enough money to pay back the loan," Rachid observed. "There's not enough business in the *souk* to match the tearoom's profits."

"Could we deliver bread and pastries to enough restaurants and hotels to meet our debt?" I asked.

"Leila, I know you'd be willing to work day and night to keep us alive," Walid said, placing his hand on mine, "but we could never prepare enough food and get it distributed to enough clients with only one truck and one driver. Perhaps it could be done if we had time to plan, find a larger kitchen and hire additional bakers and drivers. That would, however, be a completely new business."

"And," Rachid replied, "you'd need to apply for licenses that would be rejected by an invisible official whose name we cannot learn."

We were all silent for a time. Amin, who stood in the door, asked what would happen if we couldn't find another location.

"We'll lose everything," Walid said calmly. "Not only the tearoom, but the bank will probably take our old bakery and apartment to cover the debt."

"And I suspect," Khalil added, "you'll find it impossible to rent another apartment anywhere in Casablanca."

I was suddenly aware of the traffic on the street outside. The baby, wrapped in a sling against my breasts, stirred in her sleep. Beside me Walid watched her, his troubled eyes filled with love.

"I don't know what would happen to Mother if she had to leave her home," Hania said. "She's lived in that apartment for over thirty years."

"You can live with us," Rachid said, looking at Walid and me. "Our place isn't large, but we'll find a way."

"I have an idea," Aisha said in a tentative voice. "I've been thinking about this for a few weeks, but I wasn't sure until now you'd even consider it.

"Please listen to everything I have to say. I know you'll think it impossible at first, but this may be an acceptable solution." She placed her hands flat on the tabletop.

"Before Fatima and I returned from France, we lived in the seventeenth *arrondisement* in Paris. It's an area where many people from our world shop and work, and our customs and values are respected by the community. If I'm not mistaken," she said, looking at Walid, "you've been there."

"I've visited Barbes," he answered.

"It might be possible for you to obtain a permit to live there."

"In France?" Rachid asked.

"In Paris," Aisha responded. "I'm trying to suggest you open a tearoom in Paris."

"A tearoom in Paris?" Walid echoed, incredulous. "We have no capital."

"There are empty businesses all over the city, but particularly in the immigrant quarters, that could be taken over by anyone willing to renovate them."

"But who would give them the money?" Hania asked.

"That's where Fatima and I come in," Aisha said. "We've met many people in Paris who want to make our neighborhoods cleaner and safer. If the French government gives you permission to live there, we would call upon the community leaders to help you obtain a lease for a bakery."

Khalil nodded. "I agree with Aisha. I think this can be done."

"But how would we get work permits? We have no special skills," Walid said.

"Actually," Khalil replied, "with your family's record of running successful bakeries for over three decades, no one would question whether you have the skills necessary to do the same in France."

"And your story is known in France," Aisha said to me, "thanks to *The Voice*. You'll have allies in the university community, as well."

Though listening to every word, I was unable to grasp that we might leave Casablanca to make our home in France. And in Paris, no less?

"There is both good and bad to this idea," Khalil now said. "Life is much more expensive in France, and immigrants are not always welcome."

"The weather is bad for much of the year," Hania added.

"And Ziri would have to attend French schools, so Berber and Arabic would be foreign languages for her," Aisha noted, "even if you continue to speak them at home."

I looked at the baby, then at Walid.

"Where would we live?" I asked Aisha.

"Many businesses have apartments attached, like your home here in Casablanca. It might not be a modern building, but it would be a start."

"I refuse to take my family to live in those areas outside the city with so much crime," Walid said.

"Of course not!," Aisha replied. "I would never recommend you live anywhere that's not safe."

"And," Khalil put in, "if you obtain the right paperwork, your mother could come with you. She could help with the baby."

"I think," Khalil continued, "that no matter how powerful the Minister and his son are in Morocco, their power will not extend as far as Paris. Even if life is more difficult in the north, you might finally be safe.

Walid looked at me. "What do you think, Leila?"

I glanced around the table.

"I'm so sorry," I said quietly. "When I stepped into the bakery eight years ago, I never guessed I would cause you all so much pain. I thank you, Aisha, Khalil and Amin, for everything you've done to help and protect us.

"I know it's too late to go back and change what's happened, so we must decide the best way to go forward. I know nothing of Paris, except what I've read in books, seen on the television, and what people have told me. But I'm willing to try."

Walid smiled, then looked back at the others. "How should we proceed?"

The following days were difficult for each of us in different ways. We all loved our tearoom, and to close it felt like the death of our dream. The building owner extended our lease for three months, more for his own profit than out of kindness, which gave us time to sell our belongings and prepare to leave the country. I don't know how he excused himself to Essaouira.

The immigration process was complicated and confusing. Finding the documents necessary to prove our citizenship, proof of marriage, education, criminal history, tax status, financial responsibility, and health history took time, patience and effort. Often our forms were returned because some small detail had been overlooked, or answered incorrectly.

Though I'm sure my former Master knew of our plan, he did not see fit — or was perhaps unwilling to face the scrutiny he would have brought upon himself — if he pressed formal charges against me. As such, there was no official record of my arrest, incarceration, interrogation, or even suspicion that I had ever committed a crime, to impede my request for a work permit from the French government.

Perhaps the article about my years in Essaouira stayed the Minister's hand. Or perhaps — and I would never know — Young Mistress played a role in our freedom.

Walid and I spoke openly and honestly to Selina on the very same night of the meeting at the bookstore. We explained what was happening to the tearoom, and what Aisha had suggested. Selina listened gravely, green eyes moving between our faces. She then touched her granddaughter's soft curls.

"So you're telling me Ziri will learn to speak French instead of Berber?" she asked.

"Of course, not," I said. "We would speak to her in Berber every day!"

"And she'll never eat a good *tagine*! The French don't eat anything except fried potatoes and chicken!"

"She'd be living in a business with a very big kitchen," Walid responded, joining in. "We'd make sure to serve her *tagine* as well as lentil soup."

"Pardon me, my son — Leila is an excellent baker, and you are a wonderful accountant, but no one makes lentil soup as good as mine!"

"This is true, Mother," I said. "It would be very difficult for us without your lentil soup."

"And who would teach her to swim? There are no beaches in Paris!"

"We will go to a swimming pool," Walid replied, "though no pool can match our blue waters."

"And how will she learn our mountain songs, with no one to sing with Leila?"

"You're right," I agreed. "Our songs were meant to be sung with others."

Walid rose from the table. "We can speak about this tomorrow, if you'd like some time to think."

"Do you — do you think other mountain people live in this neighborhood in Paris?" Selina asked.

Walid stopped at the door. "Yes, Mother, I do."

"Well," she said quietly, "I want to help you take care of little Ziri."

"And the bakery —?"

Selina sighed and looked around the room filled with photographs of our family. For a moment her expression was lost in the sea of memory that crowded the small space. "I have lived a full life here, and yes, it will be difficult to leave. But the soul of these rooms is not their past: it is in the people who lived here. What purpose would I have here without you?"

"Mother, you can remain in Casablanca, with Hania and Rachid," Walid said.

"Yes, and I will visit them as often as I can. But I think it's little Ziri who needs me, now." She smiled. "And after all: I have always wanted to see *la Tour Eiffel*!"

17.   THE NEW VILLAGE

The Rue Gabrielle is one of the oldest streets in Paris. It winds steep and curving from the base of Montmartre, near the funicular that takes visitors up the tall hill to the white-domed church of Sacre Coeur. Our new business, a café-bakery called *Ziri*, is placed at a smooth bend in the street, at the foot of a long, steep stairway.

We are very, very busy. Tourists from many countries, drawn by the extraordinary view of Paris from the heights of Montmartre, wander the courtyard filled with artists, and find themselves standing at the top of the steep stairs overlooking our street. Many descend the stairs, arriving directly in front of our door. Inside they find a large room lit by stained-glass lanterns, and filled with wide cushions and low brass tables. The windows are thrown open, sending scents of mint tea, Moroccan coffee, warm butter croissants, and fresh honeyed pastries, far and wide.

It is rare that our tables are not full, even in winter. I work in the kitchen alongside our apprentice bakers — three young women from a trade program in Paris. Walid assists Selina and two young men, who are also students, in serving our customers. Our daughter is in school during the day, and attends art and sports programs in the late afternoon. She is happy, and speaks Berber and Arabic, as well as French. Walid and I have started learning English at night.

We live in an apartment above the café. The building, over two hundred years old, has high ceilings and tall windows that brighten the rooms, even on the many rainy days. We arrived with little more than the clothes and photographs we could pack in a few suitcases, but Fatima and

Aisha's friends had furnished the flat with tables and beds. Little by little, we have made it our home.

On warm nights Walid and I often climb the steep stairs to the heights of Montmartre. We stand on the stone balcony and gaze out over the blue horizon of the city. Then, winding our way down the hill, we return to our home and sleep soundly, without dreams.

There are times when we speak of the Casablanca sunlight passing through the red transom, staining the white tile floor the color of blood. We laugh about the little dog that never stopped barking from the balcony across the street, and the French customers who found our *amandines* so enticing. But we never, ever speak of the gentle cajoling, sudden rages, soothing melodies and hypnotic murmurs of the sea. We simply cannot bring ourselves to talk of the much-missed moods of the sea.

We work hard, but we are together. We are safe. We are free.

We had been in France for just over a year when Khalil called to say he was visiting Paris, and wanted to spend an afternoon with us. He arrived on a Monday — the day the café was closed — and joined us for lunch in our apartment.

Though still young in appearance, Khalil now wore a neat beard, and his hair was carefully trimmed. When in Paris, he dressed as we did, in conservative European attire, and looked like a commentator on television, or a youthful member of Parliament.

As we ate he talked of the political agitation in Morocco. Many people, including students at the universities, were calling for an end to the monarchy, and the creation of a democratic state. I understood Khalil was trying to tell me that many people believed men such as my former Master were corrupt, and should be removed from power.

When our meal was finished, he asked if we'd be willing to visit some friends from his school who lived a short train ride away, in the suburbs. Selina agreed to watch Ziri, and the three of us set out, taking the noisy Metro to the Gare du Nord, then a much quieter commuter train to a place called Garges les Gonesse.

Though we traveled no more than half an hour, it seemed we had journeyed to a different world. Warehouses, abandoned factories and weed-barbed lots gave way to small brick station houses dating back to another century, and tiny homes were strewn like pebbles down narrow, stone streets. Then, rising across the horizon, we were suddenly surrounded by giant concrete structures, with hundreds of identical balconies and uncountable rows of windows.

The unpainted station was festooned with spray-painted words and symbols. Walkways strung with wire fencing turned the passage over the tracks into cages, and we followed the silent crowds that descended the train into the naked, crumbling world.

It was easy to see that most of the inhabitants were, like us, brown or black. Store windows bore placards in both French and Arabic, and most women wore the *djellaba*, and some were clad in *burkas*, revealing nothing but their eyes. Men lounged on corners, benches and in groups along the street, talking, smoking, and in most cases, drinking alcohol. The few young women on the streets walked quickly into stores, or pushed baby carriages, and made eye contact with no one. Police cars circled restlessly, like hawks hunting prey. Somewhere in the near distance we heard the sustained roar of a highway.

"What is this place?" Walid asked in a low voice.

"It is popularly called '*la cité*,'" Khalil explained, equally quietly. "The buildings are called 'HLMs,' or *habitation à loyer modéré*. Though originally intended to offer rent at lower prices to those who cannot afford to live in the city, they are, in fact, a kind of prison for immigrants who made the mistake of coming to France poor and uneducated."

I lifted my eyes to the apartment buildings. Most balconies were draped with clothing hung out to dry, despite the cool, damp air. Though the rainbows of swaying fabric might have been beautiful in a different place, here they added to the sense of overcrowding, poverty, and fear. I could hardly imagine a sadder place to be a child.

We approached a building of four or five stories, that appeared to be some sort of hospital. Metal grating covered the doors and windows. Inside, an armed guard sitting at a desk stopped us. He asked to look through my bag, and waved a sensor over our clothing to check for weapons. Khalil turned to us.

"This is my first time coming here, so please forgive me if I don't know exactly where to go."

"Why are we here?" Walid asked.

"I want to show you something. Please, give me just a few more moments and everything will be clear."

We followed him down a long, bright corridor, opening to offices in which men and women worked at desks. It was startlingly clean and quiet, compared to the streets outside.

We were directed to elevators that moved smoothly up several floors. The doors revealed a nurses' station, and a woman in light blue immediately rose to greet us.

"My name is Saidi Khalil. I spoke to you two days ago about visiting one of your patients."

The woman consulted a list and nodded without further conversation. She led us down another clean, silent corridor. This time, however, we saw large dayrooms where women watched television, worked on puzzles, or simply sat in the gray light, staring at nothing at all.

At the end of the corridor the woman addressed Khalil.

"We don't encourage visitors to stay long, unless they've been cleared by a doctor. The patients are used to their routines, and often don't do well when their schedules are changed, so please keep your visit short."

Khalil turned to me.

"Leila, when you filled out the application for a work permit, you gave us as much information about your family as you could remember. I hope you won't mind, but I took the liberty of conducting a search of government records for a woman named Mohammed Zahra Tiziri, and I found only one. The record indicated she came to France fourteen years ago with her husband, Mohammed Omar, who abandoned her because she was too ill to care for their two sons. She has been hospitalized ever since. She lives here, on this fl —"

A great roaring drowned out his words. The corridor darkened as it careened sickly and I felt Walid's arms grasp my waist to keep me from falling. From somewhere a bottle of water was placed in my trembling fingers, and when my vision cleared, I found myself on the floor with the two men and several attendants around me.

"Please," I whispered, "please help me up. I'm alright, now."

Walid helped me to my feet. The ringing pain in my hip cleared my head, and I leaned against him until I felt my balance return. Then, still trembling, I walked without assistance to the door. I looked back at Walid, who nodded once.

I entered the room alone.

I was met with the cold-metal odor of bleach. Two young women were sitting in front of a television in bathrobes, staring blankly at the screen. Their hair was cut short and they wore no shoes. A third woman, in a wheelchair, shook convulsively every few seconds. Her shaved head was lowered and her fine-boned hands were clasped in her lap.

The fourth woman sat on a folding metal chair just beside the grilled window. Long, stark white hair was twisted into a loose braid that hung down her back, past her hips. Perilously thin, I could see her shoulder blades through the cotton gown that covered her upper body. Her legs were folded at the calf and tucked beneath her seat, and her head rested heavily against the metal bars.

Very slowly, I moved a few steps closer. I could see her left lobe was cleft, cut neatly in two, where long ago her husband had torn an earring from her flesh.

Hardly breathing, feeling as if my feet no longer met the floor, I reached out to touch her, then paused, my hand suspended above her shoulder.

"Mother?" I whispered in a voice not my own.

The woman did not move.

"Mother?" I said again, this time with more strength and conviction.

She stirred, but did not turn her head.

"Mother —" tears had come into my eyes and were making their way down my cheeks.

The woman moved haltingly, her head twisting so slowly it seemed a century before she looked in my direction. She lifted her face.

The gaze was distant, lost, hollow. But the eyes were green. Apple green. She stared at the wall over my shoulder.

"Mother." The sound was the wisp of a bird's wing, the breeze on the petals of a mountain flower. *"Mother."*

All pain vanished as I slipped to my knees beside her.

Slowly she reached out, knotted fingers seeking, then finding my face. Without a sound, the blankness in her eyes filled with wounded, trembling disbelief.

Leila?

I'm alive, Mother.

You are here?

I am here, beside you.

You have found me.

I have found you.

I love you.

I love you, too. I will never go away again.

Epilogue

Somewhere I have two brothers who do not know what has become of their sister, or their mother. I am sure my father married again and has raised them with little, or no memory of the woman who fought to protect them in a dirt-floored hut in the mountains. Perhaps, if even a sliver of memory of their elder sister remains, or of the woman who gave them life, they will make an effort to find us. We have done all we can to find them.

My mother, or Henna Tizi, as baby Ziri calls her, is rediscovering her life. Though the doctors do not believe her quite well enough to release her to our care, we moved her to a smaller hospital, not far from Montmartre. We see her often, and Henna Selina spends many hours talking with her, brushing her hair, and they even go to the *hamman*, or steam baths, together. My mother smiles, sometimes laughs, and both knows and loves her namesake and granddaughter.

Often we sing. The song begins with a melody she hums to herself, cascading and climbing out of memories older even than my life. I see her looking into the days when she tied the purple scarf around her hips and danced, by moonlight, to my father's wandering flute. If I know the song I join in, and she raises her voice to welcome mine. If Selina is there, the harmony is blended once more, and our voices make their way back home. It is in song that I'm closest to my mother, and her eyes are clear and her soul is restored.

Hania has given birth to a daughter, Izza, and Rachid and the boys are delighted. We talk to them daily on our new computer, and they visit us every summer. Fatima and Aisha often stop in as they go about their work on behalf of those who have no voice. Fatima, who settled in Marseilles, married one of Khalil's classmates, and in him has a powerful ally. I write often to Madame Chafik, who sees me when she comes to Paris. And Walid still encourages me to turn my story into a book. Perhaps, when Ziri is older, I'll try.

Once, long ago, a prostitute in a house of pleasure told me that memory is the taste of lost freedom. This may be true, but my memories tell a different story: No matter how dark the night, hope must be the last thing to die.

Acknowledgements

Leila: The Weighted Silence of Memory
and
Leila II: The Moods of the Sea

The character of Leila was born in a photograph taken by Marcel Neff during our brief visit to Essaouira, Morocco, in 1985. The character, and the events of the novels chronicling her life, are pure fiction, and have no basis in any actual events. Human trafficking occurs in nearly every nation on earth, and is not limited to any specific race, religion, nationality or ethnic group.

I depended on *Moroccan Cooking*, by Latifa Bennani-Smires for the detailed descriptions of Moroccan cuisine, and gleaned the proverbs used in these novels from several sources, including the website: http://www.whirlitzer.org/berbersay.html .

These books owe much to the detailed editing of Laurie Walker, whose creativity and kindness are matched by her instinctual understanding of the author's blindness. I am especially thankful for her encouragement, for Leila's story was often painful to conceive, and even more difficult to write.

Though I am daily strengthened by the support of my students, colleagues, readers, and friends, I thank my daughter and my mother, in particular, for inspiring me — in the words of W.E.B. du Bois — to forever seek my "better and truer self."

Heather Mayson Neff

33467900R00143

Made in the USA
Charleston, SC
15 September 2014